Cougar Adventurers Edition

This Tomser Cat Book Belongs To:

_____

_____

See if you can spot Tomser Cat
hiding somewhere in the pages of this book!

For
Rhiannon
who sleeps under the Mountain

First published in 2016 by Tomser Cat Books
Ty Mawr House
Bryn Henwysg
Troedrhiw-Trwyn
Pontypridd CF37 2SE

www.tomsercat.com

A CIP catalogue record for this book is available from the British
Library

ISBN: 978-0-9927621-5-5

Printed in Great Britain

The Mystery
of the

and the

Great Deep Sleep
Miscalculation

Mark Dorey

illustrated by Liz Dorey

Cougar Adventurers Edition

Tomser Cat Books

The Mystery of the Un-Snowy Mountain and the Great Deep Sleep Miscalculation

Dragon Appendix:

A Brief History of Dragons

Many thanks to

Gary for all his support and advice

A Dragon
is to be
Admired and Feared
in equal measure
but
under no circumstances
Ignored

Chancer proverb

Chapter One

SOMETHING VERY STRANGE...

"There's something very strange about that mountain," said Grandpa, his voice low and even more gravelly than usual as he stared out of the window at the mountain in the distance. Tyler joined his gaze, the nine-year-old bursting with curiosity.

"What is it, Gramps?" he asked, his eyes alight with expectation.

Grandpa leant forward, their noses almost touching. "Can you keep a secret?"

Tyler's head bobbed up and down so fast that it was in danger of falling off!

"Snow," said Grandpa, his voice barely a whisper.

"Snow?" echoed Tyler.

"Snow," repeated Grandpa, "or rather, the lack of it."

Tyler was confused.

Grandpa's eyes widened beneath bushy silver-grey eyebrows arching to the top of his bald head. "When it snows, the Mountain will reveal its secret."

Tyler's chin dropped. "Aw, can't you tell me now?"

Grandpa smiled a sad-and-not-quite-a-smile sort of smile that Tyler had never seen before. "Patience, Tyler lad, patience."

"But Gramps—"

There was a knock on the door.

"Looks like your mother's here."

Tyler sighed. Now he'd never get to the bottom of the snow mystery. "See you next week then," he said, trying not to sound too disappointed.

"I'll be here," said Grandpa.

Tyler swung open the door, shivering as the chill wintry air snapped at his skin like an invisible frost monster.

His Mum peered over his shoulder. "You okay, Dad?"

"Fine, love," said Grandpa.

"Thanks for looking after him. We've got to rush, but I'll pop back over tomorrow. Come on, Tyler, wrap up warm. It's cold enough for snow."

Snow!

Tyler's spirits lifted as he pulled on his coat, hat and scarf before scampering over to give his Gramps a goodbye hug. Grandpa ruffled a calloused hand through his grandson's browny-orange spiky mop. The old man's smile vanished into the depths of his beard as soon as the door closed behind his grandson.

"There's something strange about that mountain..." he said to no one in particular.

Tyler's house was ten minutes walk from his Grandpa's.

"Mum, is Grandpa all right?"

"He's not too bad, although he can't get about like he used to." Her piercing blue eyes probed her son, looking for hidden secrets. "Why do you ask?" her steamy breath billowed on the frosty air.

"No reason," he tried to sound casual, but inside Tyler was bursting to ask her if she knew anything about the mountain and the snow; after all, Mum had grown up in the village.

They walked in silence for a bit before Mum spoke again. "It's quite difficult for him, you know, especially since Grandma died."

Tyler nodded. It had been difficult for him too. Visiting his grandparents was always something Tyler looked forward to, with lots of fun, laughter and games. But best by far had been the stories. Grandpa was the best storyteller in the whole world but the stories stopped when Grandma died.

Everything stopped.

Grandma was gone. All that was left was her picture in a little silver frame on the mantelpiece above the fire, and

Grandma's old walking stick with its red-brown coppery head.

The ornately carved walking stick leant sadly against the back door, as if waiting for her return, and no one, but no one was allowed to touch it.

Tyler and his family had moved to just outside Rudry village to be close to Grandpa. But even two years on, things were never quite the same. Always a person with a love for the Great Outdoors, Grandpa now rarely left the house.

"Don't worry, love, things will be all right," Mum draped a comforting arm over his shoulder.

Tyler nodded but said nothing, his thoughts filled with lost Grandmas, lost stories and a Grandpa full of secrets...

The stars glittered like diamonds on a blanket of night as the Dragon soared across the sky. Clouds loomed on the horizon waiting to pounce. He would have to be quick. The white of the clouds would blow his cover. The Dragon only ventured out on moonless nights and when he did, it was for one thing: **FOOD!**

But this Dragon didn't hunt for sheep or cattle that might have strayed in the night. No, that would be unthinkable! When this Dragon went hunting, he would scour the countryside for... FRUIT!

The Dragon plummeted out of the sky like a huge black dart towards a garden allotment with a large greenhouse. Someone moved in the darkness below. Someone was standing guard outside his greenhouse. A lot of fruit had gone missing over the past few months...

High above the Dragon circled and smiled. He loved this game! Drawing in a deep breath, the Dragon heated the cold air deep inside his fiery body. Seconds later, he breathed out sending smoky rings drifting down over the unsuspecting night watchman. Within a few seconds the greenhouse guard was fast asleep, still standing bolt upright! The giant beast chuckled with delight. He breathed some more Dragon Magic, this time wispy strands of smoke, weaved and danced as they wrapped around the handle of the greenhouse door, opening it without a sound.

This was going to be easy!

The smoky strands split into octopus-like tentacles, wrapping around all kinds of fruit - bananas, pineapples, oranges, nectarines, melons, tomatoes, mangoes and the Dragon's favourite, strawberries! (He always avoided lemons as he found that they gave him terrible wind and a very bad tummy!)

The Dragon licked his lips, his belly gurgling and popping like an old steam engine.

Not long now...

The bobbing line of fruit snaked silently out of the greenhouse, rising up towards the hovering Dragon, who was eagerly awaiting the captured bounty. Then disaster! The last piece of fruit, a large pineapple caught the doorframe and toppled free.

SPLAT

CRASH

BANG!

BANG! A CLONK!

SMASH!

The pineapple clattered into a stack of empty pots. The spell broken, the sleeping gardener sprang awake, his eyes growing wide as the stolen fruit bobbed past on a wispy conveyor belt of magical smoke up into the night sky. The startled man's eyes grew wider still as he followed the fruity trail skywards...

There, filling the darkness was a huge

D-D-D-D-DRAGON!

The Dragon looked at the man.

The man looked at the Dragon.

The man promptly fainted face down in a bed of cabbages!

"Oh dear," sighed the Dragon.

The wispy strand closed the glass door as the hovering Dragon gathered in the last of the fruit. Letting out a long breath, the Dragon bathed the whole greenhouse in **blue-pink** Dragon Magic. Then, in an instant, everything returned to darkness.

The Dragon was gone.

Seconds later, the gardener stirred, sat up and looked around.

He'd had the strangest dream...

What was it...?

No, it couldn't have been...

Brushing off the squashed cabbage leaves, he opened the greenhouse door. The most wonderful fruity smell filled the air. Broken pots littered the floor. More fruit had gone missing. But far from being empty, the greenhouse was laden with fruit...

He scratched his head, sighing as he picked up the broken pieces. "Ah well, I suppose I could always enter them into the *Largest Fruit Competition*."

And that's what he did - winning the *Largest Fruit Prize* in every category.

Of course, he never told anyone what happened. After all, who would believe him?

---

[1] If the Dragon Magic made the fruit bigger, then why didn't the Dragon simply take less fruit and use Dragon Magic to make it bigger for himself to eat? The answer is that the fruit, even though it may look bigger and feel heavier, the increase in size and weight is in fact an illusion, and so would not fill the Dragon up any more than 'un-Dragon-Magic-ed' fruit!

The Dragon entered his secret lair deep under Rudry Mountain, heaping his fruity hoard on to a large mound already piled high on the cavern floor.

"Now, what shall I cook tonight?" A rumble escaped from the depths of his tummy. "Oh, do be quiet! Now, let me see, maybe some roast pineapple stuffed with bananas and strawberries, or smoked tomatoes covered in a light barbecue sauce made from mango juice, or perhaps... both! Yes, yes, yes, both, with some fresh strawberries topped with a dusting of seared orange peel for dessert - Perfect!"

The Dragon started to prepare his fruity concoctions. There were times that he would feel a little peckish for something other than fruit, something different. But as he could never figure out exactly what that *something* was, he stuck with his fruit diet.

Meanwhile, outside his mountain lair it

started to snow!

Chapter Two

THE GREAT DEEP SLEEP
MISCALCULATION

Now, if you know anything at all about Dragons, there may well be some rather perplexing Dragony questions bouncing around inside your Dragon curious and slightly befuddled head:

Dragony Question 1

How did the Dragon come to be living under Rudry Mountain in the first place?

Dragony Question 2

Why did he like eating fruit and nothing else - surely this must go against many Dragon protocols?

11

Dragony Question 3

Do all Dragons live under mountains, eating strange assortments of fruit, or more importantly still (especially if they eat other things as well), are there any living under a mountain close to my house?

For those of you who don't know that much about Dragons and would like to know a little more about their various types and characters, please read the Dragon Appendix: *A Brief History of Dragons* at the back of this book.[2] But in order to answer those more immediate Dragony questions, you need to know about one of the Earth's oldest secrets...

The Great Deep Sleep Miscalculation!

Many thousands of years ago, a great Ice Age swept across the Earth. It happened very quickly and a lot of creatures caught out by the sudden climate change unfortunately became extinct. The Dragons (who were extremely clever and saw these changes coming), realised that they would have to do something until the Ice Age was over in order to survive the bitter cold. Even the cold-loving Blue Dragons were worried at the prospect of an Ice Age, which caused even greater alarm amongst all Dragonkind.

A Grand Dragon Council was called and all the Dragons were summoned. Such was the importance of the meeting

---

[2] When you see a § in a footnote, it means more information is available in the *A Brief History of Dragons* Appendix at the end of this book.

that even the nasty and unruly Red Dragons were ordered to attend. After much debate, it was agreed that all the Dragons would go into a magical 'Deep Sleep' encased in Dragon Magic stone until the Ice Age was over.

It was decided that the best place for the 'Deep Sleep' would be in the highest and deepest mountains situated in what we now know as North Wales.[3] After the Council meeting all the Dragons migrated North to hide themselves deep in the Snowdonia mountains and make preparations for their mass hibernation.

Complex calculations for determining how long the Ice Age would last were left to the Silver Dragons who were considered to be the cleverest. They calculated that the impending Cold Snap would last for 8,167 years, give or take a month or two. Everyone agreed it would be a good idea to round up the 'Deep Sleep' spell to 10,000 years, so that everything would have time to thaw out and Mother Nature could get her act back together. Unfortunately, in the rush and confusion of the last minute preparations (and a skirmish breaking out between a number of Black and Red Dragons, who were prone to fooling around and generally making nuisances of themselves), a small but significant error was made in the 'Deep Sleep' calculation. An extra '0' was accidentally added, meaning that the spell was cast for 100,000 years by mistake!

---

[3] For reasons why Wales was chosen in particular, see *A Brief History of Dragons* (if you have not already done so). §

A final count was made to ensure that all Dragons were present and correct,[4] all of them completely unaware of this catastrophic error. Then the powerful Dragon Magic of the Deep Sleep spell was cast, transforming all the Dragons into solid stone deep within the Welsh mountains - all the Dragons that is, except one. One Dragon was unfortunately overlooked because at the time of the Great Spell casting, he was still an Egg; a white-coated egg that was missed in the falling of the ancient snows of long, long ago.

No one thought to include any Dragon Eggs in the count because the Dragon Egg-Laying Season was over.[5] During this time all the Dragons had laid their eggs, including this Dragon's Mother, who laid five Dragon Eggs - of which his was the last. After the incubation period, all the eggs had hatched successfully apart from one, who showed no sign of hatching even after a few extra months of careful incubation.

With the threat of the impending Ice Age looming ever closer, the Dragon Doctor suggested they try the uncommon

---

[4] Green Dragons decided they did not want to be part of the Deep Sleep and so left before the Great Dragon Magic was cast. §

[5] The Dragon Egg-Laying season starts on the first Full Moon after the Spring Equinox and ends on the last Full Moon of the Autumn Equinox. This only occurs on a twelve year cycle, which is thought to have something to do with the orbit of the planet Jupiter. This may seem like an awfully long time between Egg-Laying seasons, but Dragons never seem too bothered about it as they age very slowly and live for a very long time.

practice known as *H.A.T.C.H.* (*Heat And Thermal Coaxing Hatching*), which involved gently warming the un-hatched egg on specially heated coals. Before any warming could take place, the precious egg was carefully wrapped in masses of orange and banana skins, followed by the further copious wrapping of lots and lots of coconut leaves around the outside. This was to protect the un-hatched Dragon from becoming too hot, too quickly from the warming coals.

The *H.A.T.C.H.* process is a dangerous procedure not often used by Dragons for a number of reasons:

1. If the egg is not wrapped in enough protective fruit skins, it will get too hot and the poor un-hatched Dragon will be poached inside. Conversely, too much wrapping stops the heat getting to the egg and the poor un-hatched Dragon eventually dies inside the shell, as Draglets (baby Dragons) can only survive for a maximum of six months once fully formed.

2. In cooler climates like Wales, to give just one example, these exotic fruit cannot be grown locally (remember, this is before greenhouses were invented). Therefore, the Father Dragon has to fly to warmer, exotic countries to bring back the necessary egg-packaging fruit materials.

3. Bringing all these exotic fruits into the Dragon's lair has the unfortunate effect of filling the inside of the mountain with a fragrant fruity smell, which unfortunately for Dragons is like the smell of mouldy rotten socks!

At the time of the *Great Dragon Migration*, the Dragon egg's Mother, Father, and four siblings hastily prepared to move out from their lair deep inside Rudry Mountain to head for the mountains of North Wales. The egg was unwrapped and nestled amongst the rest of the Dragon family's precious treasures, balanced on the Father's massive scaly back. During 'take off' the egg toppled unseen into the snow, quickly becoming invisible amidst the falling snowflakes.[6] When the Dragon family got to North Wales they had no idea of their unfortunate loss, entering the 'Deep Sleep' hibernation assuming that their unborn son was still with them.

Meanwhile, in the lower foothills of South Wales lay the abandoned egg containing the 'newly-orphaned' Dragon getting **colder...** and

COLDER...

and

COLDER...

---

[6] Dragon Eggs usually reflect the colour of the little Draglet inside. For example, Gold eggs = Gold Dragons; Silver eggs = Sliver Dragons, etc. This un-hatched egg was still coated in white baked-on ash formed as part of the H.A.T.C.H. process, masking its Bronze colour. White Dragon eggs are very rare, as are White Dragons. §

C-R-R-A-A-C-K!

The freezing cold snow caused the egg to fracture. Now, once a Dragon egg begins to hatch, a whole sequence of events are set in motion, as the tiny Draglet breaks free to begin its life in the Great World.

When this baby Dragon finally hatched out of his shell he was alone.

Alone in a vast sea of white nothingness.

What's more, he was being splattered and covered with strange cold white flaky things falling down on him from the sky above.

His fledgling Dragon instincts told him that this wasn't right; it wasn't right at all.

Everything was white – well, almost everything - the mountain next to him refused to turn white, regardless of how much of the white cold wet flaky stuff fell on to it. More importantly still, there was warmth coming from the inside of the mountain.

Now, Dragons have amazing eyesight and can see things invisible to others. Things magically hidden away from all other living creatures.

Firstly, they can see their precious Treasure. Dragons are extremely jealous of their Treasure and use ancient Dragon Magic to hide it away from everyone, including other sneaky Treasure-seeking Dragons. Most Dragons respect the lairs of other Dragons, except Black and Red Dragons, who 'like to visit' while their owners are not at home, pilfering free food or better still, unguarded Treasure.[7] For those Dragons who have not protected their Treasure with Hiding Magic, it is all too easy to find even in the darkest of corners of their lair because of the invading Dragon's phenomenal eyesight. If the Treasure is magically concealed, then the intruder has no chance of finding it because it will remain invisible to all but their owners.

---

[7] Black and Red Dragons take great pleasure in making off with Treasure belonging to other Dragons, insisting that they are only 'borrowing'.

Secondly, the entrances to Dragon lairs are magically hidden - not to other Dragons, but to other animals, particularly humans. This is so that we don't catch them sleeping and try to kill them or cause them mischief. Humans have a nasty tendency to want to kill Dragons, using their scales as armour and carrying their teeth around as trophies. Dragons understand this fact all too well.

Having spotted the magically hidden entrance to his Family's deserted lair, the newly orphaned Dragon entered the cosy warmth and security of the inside of the mountain. His family had taken all their food with them for their trip North, but had abandoned all the fruit that had been collected for the failed *H.A.T.C.H.* process. The little Draglet knew nothing of eating sheep and cows that a normal Dragon might feast on, but he did know that he was hungry. Very, very hungry. So when he found himself faced with small mountains of discarded fruit, he simply tucked in, and because he never knew any different, fruit became his diet from then on.

This all happened many thousands of years ago, and since then the world had changed a lot. The Ice Age came and went in less than 9,000 years, (as the Dragons had correctly predicted), and this last Dragon spent most of this time hibernating and eating small bits of fruit until the warmer climate returned.[8]

---

[8] Obviously fruit cannot last 9,000 years in its natural state, unless it is carefully preserved with Dragon Magic.

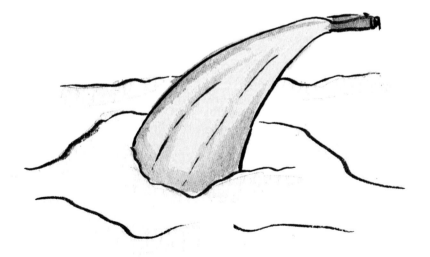

Chapter Three

HALF A BANANA!

Snow fell heavily that wintry Saturday morning. For the first time in years everywhere was covered in a glistening blanket of snowy white. Everywhere that is, except Rudry Mountain. For some strange reason, snow never *ever* settled on the Mountain. Some thought it was magic; others said the Mountain was simply made up of hot rock. But the truth lay somewhere in between.

Tyler's Dad looked out of the window with boyish excitement. Racing into the hallway, he shouted up the stairs. "Come on, Tyler, it's time for some tobogganing!"

Tyler, still half-submerged beneath his cosy warm bedclothes and desperately not wanting to do anything, pulled the covers resolutely over his head.

"Come on, Tyler, quick, before the snow melts!"

Tyler didn't care about the stupid snow, all he cared about was staying in his lovely warm—

Something clicked in Tyler's head.

Something his Gramps had said.

'When it snows, the Mountain will reveal its secret!'

Tyler was up and dressed in under two minutes. Scooting downstairs he hastily munched through some last-minute toast, and with his breakfast barely settled, they headed outdoors, clad in boots, woolly hats, scarves and gloves. As they set off with their toboggan in tow, Tyler was deep in thought, wondering what the Mountain's secret could be. As they rounded the bend, the Mountain came into view - an island of green in a sea of white, with not so much as a snowflake settled anywhere on its surface.

Was this it, the Mountain's big un-snowy secret?

Tyler stared gloomily at the lush green pasture of the Mountain as his Dad stood and stared, his eyes nearly popping out of his head! Then Dad was off, tossing his gloves aside as he reached the grassy slopes. Scrambling about on his hands and knees, Dad's lanky frame wriggled over the grass like a frantic caterpillar.

"It's not frozen," Dad prodded everywhere desperate to discover the Mountain's secret.

By the time Tyler caught up, Dad had his ear to the ground, his eyebrows moving up and down in a slow rhythmic dance as he listened intently. Then, with a shake of the head, off came his woolly hat as he pressed his head once again into the grass.

"Dad—"

"SSSHHH!" Dad listened intently for several minutes before scrambling to his feet. Barely able to keep still, his curls of browny-orange hair bobbed with a springy life all their own. "I need to get some instruments. Tyler, you stay here. I'll just be a few minutes."

Why would Dad want to play his instruments on a cold winter's morning at the foot of a boringly un-snowy Mountain?

Before he could say anything, Dad raced off. Tyler scuffed the grass with his foot. Grown-ups sure were strange sometimes.

He glared at the Mountain.

Stupid secret.

Trudging back down to where the snow had stopped, Tyler considered his options, but basically there was only one. The disgruntled nine-year-old began rolling and piling snow into a snowman's body. The head quickly followed. Before long Tyler was standing next to his first solo-built snowman - a fine effort, even if the snowman was still naked and faceless.

Dad returned, barely breaking his stride as he hiked past with armfuls of weird items, and not a single musical instrument in sight.

"Well done, Tyler lad. Great job!"

Tyler scoured the snow retrieving stones to make the snowman's eyes, mouth and buttons before standing back to admire his work.

Something wasn't quite right.

Taking off his scarf, he draped it around the snowman's neck.

Better, but there was still something else missing...

A Nose!

The snowman needed a nose; a stone was no good - not quite nosey enough.

A carrot – he needed a carrot.

How was he ever going to find a carrot in all this snow?

He needed help.

Tyler scrunched his eyes and made a wish, and just to underline the urgency, he finished with a solemn "Amen". Then he set about looking for the hidden nose, starting his search where the green grass of the Mountain ended and the snow began. Spreading his arms and fanning them out like windscreen wipers, Tyler worked at clearing away the layers of snow until he could see the fresh grass underneath. After several exhausting minutes, his arms were aching and his hands numb even through thick winter gloves.

Maybe his *'Quest for the Missing Nose'* was a lost cause.

Suddenly, his hand hit something.

Not just any old something - a nose-shaped something.

Tyler cleared away the snow.

There in the grass was half a banana.

Half a banana sticking out of the ground!

How very strange!

Not quite a carrot, but a good nose substitute nonetheless. Taking hold of the banana, he gave it a yank. The banana remained rooted in the ground but Tyler was not about to give up. Sitting with one foot either side of the banana, he took hold again and pulled with all his might.

Something moved - not the banana - his feet.

His feet began to *sink into the Mountain!*

Tyler panicked, releasing the banana, and toppling backwards. Gathering himself, he crawled back on all fours to examine the ground where his feet were moments before.

Nothing.

Not even footprints.

Just un-trodden grass.

Tyler pushed down with his hands to get back to his feet. His hands sank into the Mountain like he was pressing

25

against a giant grass-covered sponge. Pulling his hands back, Tyler checked his fingers. Good, none missing. Once again, he pressed down into the grass. Once again, his hands sank into the side of the Mountain.

This needed investigating.

Yanking off his woolly hat, Tyler pressed his head against the grass.

Nothing.

He pressed a little harder.

The ground started to give way.

Closing his eyes, Tyler pushed harder and further, his head popping through the inside of the Mountain as if he were pulling on a new Christmas sweater.

Tyler opened his eyes. It was dark, but not completely dark. He was in a tunnel, or at least his head was. Tyler pulled backwards until he was back outside the Mountain.

His Dad was nowhere to be seen.

Tyler reclaimed his scarf. "Sorry, Mr Snowy, but I need to borrow this for a bit. It's time for a little exploring."

The snowman stared back unblinking with a fixed smile.

"Keep watch until I get back."

The snowman again said nothing, but was still smiling, so Tyler took this to mean 'Okay'.

Checking that no one was around, he pushed his way back into the Mountain, trailing his scarf behind him so that he would be able to find his way back out through the secret entrance.

Chapter Four

INSIDE THE MOUNTAIN

The tunnel was gloomy but warm – very warm. Tyler discarded his coat next to the other half of the banana laying on the floor in the dim half light. Up ahead, he could see the tunnel widening as it gradually got brighter. The warning hairs on the back of his neck stood up, urging him

to retreat, but something greater told him he needed to explore. Taking a deep breath, Tyler ventured down the tunnel towards the growing eerie light. The further along he went, the more he could hear something - a low rattling noise. He peered over his shoulder back towards the concealed entrance, his scarf and coat now barely visible in the gloom.

Tyler pressed on, the rattling becoming louder and deeper with every step. Occasionally he would come across a stray piece of fruit on the rocky floor which he dutifully picked up, until soon he was carrying a whole armful of fruity debris. Then unexpectedly, the tunnel exploded out into a huge cave. He had explored lots of caves with his Dad (Dad was some kind of *geo-logic* person), but Tyler had never seen anything like this.

The huge cavern was filled with a strange bluey-greeny-slightly-purpley light that radiated from its walls. Unlike the chilly cold of other caves Tyler had visited, this one was toasty warm. At its centre, a large bonfire blazed, a variety of fruit-laden spits

made out of tree branches slowly roasting above the flames. Waves of delicious barbecuey fruity smells wafted on the air, filling the whole cavern with a mouth-watering-fruitastic aroma!

It was a wonderful sight, but by far the biggest wonder, the most eye-popping-dangerous-wonder that took Tyler's breath away, lay just beyond the fruity barbecue. There, right before his eyes, was a great sleeping Dragon, its bronze scales coming alive in the dancing flames of the barbecue.

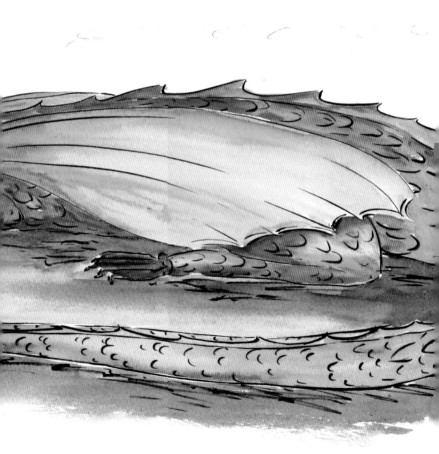

As tall as a double-decker bus and many times as long, the magnificent creature lay, its long, winding tail twitching with every resounding snore as trails of smoke snaked from his elongated snout with a loud rattling noise.

Tyler froze, hoping that Dragons didn't have good hearing, but just in case they did, he held his breath. His heart was hammering in his chest. If it beat any harder, it might come flying out of his mouth and hit the sleeping Dragon bang on the nose!

Tyler clamped his mouth shut. With his eyes fixed firmly on the Dragon, he edged backwards through the tunnel...

Slowly... slowly... s-l-o-w-l-y...

Disaster struck. Tyler slipped on a stray banana skin. Time went into slow motion as the terrified youngster struggled to regain his footing.

CRUNCH!

The fruit that Tyler was carrying spilt everywhere as he hit the floor.

Tyler looked on in horror as a peach flew up in the air high above the sleeping Dragon.

The peach hit the Dragon square on the nose!
Tyler was in trouble.

BIG, BIG TROUBLE!

The rhythmic snoring of the sleeping Dragon stopped. One huge eye creaked open, peering like a giant yellow-orange searchlight, closely followed by another probing orb. The Dragon's eyes grew larger and larger. Tyler gulped the biggest gulp that he'd ever gulped as his legs turned to wobbly jelly.

He's going to eat me!

The Dragon drew back on his haunches, wings spreading wide, filling the far side of the cave. A cavernous mouth yawned open, revealing large, yellowy-brown, terrible teeth.

'Move, legs, move!'

Tyler's horrified legs refused to obey as a tidal wave of numbing terror and helplessness rooted his feet to the spot.

He was doomed.

Tyler closed his eyes wishing for it all to be a dream: the un-snowy Mountain; the half banana; the secret lair; and the enormous Tyler-eating Dragon...

He scrunched his eyes even tighter, hoping this might transport him safely to his nice warm bed.

Tyler could still hear the crackle of the bonfire.

He scrunched his eyes more than he'd ever scrunched before.

Pungent fruity smells still tickled Tyler's nose.

Other than that, nothing.

Maybe the Dragon was gone.

Taking a long deep breath, Tyler forced open one eye.

The Dragon was still there, but not as Tyler expected.

Far from being about to eat him, the huge beast was cowering in the corner.

"W-W-What do you want?"

The trembling Dragon's voice filled the cavern, fanning the flickering flames of the bonfire.

"N-N-Nothing!" Tyler replied.

"Nothing?" The Dragon's eyes narrowed.

Tyler shook his head vigorously. "No, nothing at all."

The Dragon growled, a deep grating growl that echoed around the walls, flaring the bonfire and toppling some of the fruit from atop of the fruity mound.

Tyler braced himself.

"Excuse me," said the Dragon apologetically. "I haven't eaten for quite a while."

Tyler's heart stopped.

"Would you care to join me?" The Dragon looked the boy up and down.

"W-W-What do... what do you mean?" stuttered Tyler.

"For a bite to eat."

"Me? You can't, I taste awful!"

"You?" the Dragon drew back, appalled. "Why would I want to eat you?" The Dragon turned towards the bonfire. "I just thought you might be hungry too."

"You mean... you want me to join you?"

The Dragon nodded.

"To eat... fruit?"

The Dragon nodded again. "Unless of course, you'd rather not?" The booming question hung in the air.

"Awesome!" beamed a relieved Tyler.

"Would that be a Yes or a No?" enquired the Dragon.

"It's a Yes. Thanks, er, Mr Dragon," replied Tyler.

"Mr Dragon? I haven't been called 'Mr Dragon' before. Come to think of it, I haven't been called *anything* before."

"You mean, you don't have a name?"

"A name?" pondered the Dragon. "I do have a Dragon name, it's *SHHRRRAAAAHHH-GWLLOSS-GWANNEG-GASS-SSALL*." [9]

---

[9] Dragon names tend to be very unpronounceable, and with very few exceptions are very, very long and filled with meaning known only to Dragons themselves. Coincidentally, this is in common with a lot of Welsh town names, which, if you're not Welsh can seem very

"I'm not sure that I can remember that," said Tyler. "Can I call you something else?"

"Certainly," replied the Dragon, "except for Mr Dragon, that's far too formal."

Tyler thought for a bit. "How about something a bit more Welsh. Maybe something a little more Rudry-ish?" Tyler rolled the sound around in his mouth, over and over. "Rudry... Ridry... Rhydrian... Rhydian.[10] That's it, Rhydian - Rhydian the Dragon!"

"Hmmm..." mused the Dragon, "Rhydian..." The Dragon repeated the name a few times. "Yes, yes, I like the sound of that. How very exciting! This is all very much of a surprise – well, this whole thing's a bit of a surprise - I was sleeping and I didn't expect you. In fact, you're my first ever visitor, Master...?"

"Tyler," replied Tyler. "Tyler Bradley."

---

complicated and unpronounceable indeed, particularly the longest and most famous of all: *Llanfairpwllgwyngyllgogerychwyrndrobwllllantysilio-gogogoch* (which translates as 'St Mary's church in the hollow of the white hazel near to the fierce whirlpool and the church of St Tysilio of the red cave'). To make things a bit easier, this tongue-twisting town is sometimes shortened to *Llanfairpwllgwyngyll* or *Llanfairpwll*, but as this is still something of a tongue-twisting mouthful, especially for non-Welsh speakers, it is often shortened further to *Llanfair PG*. This village with a very large name can be found on the island of Anglesey, just off the North Wales coast.

[10] A Welsh name (pronounced 'Rid-ian'), meaning 'red' or 'crimson'.

"Welcome to my home, Master Tyler Bradley!" boomed Rhydian.

Tyler smiled. "You can call me Tyler, if you like!"

"Tyler Iffulike? Is that another one of your names?"

Tyler chuckled. "No, silly, it's just Tyler!"

If Tyler had realised that he'd called his first ever Dragon 'silly', he definitely wouldn't have said it, but fortunately, neither he nor the Dragon noticed this little slip.

"Tyler it is then," said Rhydian. "Well, Tyler, would you like to help yourself to some food?"

Tyler took one of the smaller branches from the edge of the bonfire skewered with pieces of barbecued fruit. Waiting a few moments for it to cool, he cautiously took a small bite out of the hot fruit, which melted in his mouth like syrup. Tyler ate hungrily as the fruit cooled. Rhydian, grabbing a whole skewer, downed the lot in one go without even blowing on it!

A huge belch thundered from the Dragon's stomach, erupting in a volcano of smelly burp-gas, which promptly exploded in a huge blue flame high above Tyler's head!

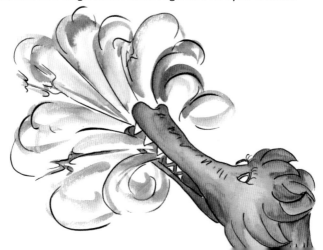

If it were possible for a Dragon to go red with embarrassment (if not already a Red Dragon that is), then Rhydian did, even though he was a Bronze Dragon.[11]

"Oops, sorry," said Rhydian, spearing some more fruit and gently cooking it with a spiral of blue-green flame, before offering it to Tyler.

Tyler took it gratefully and tucked in.

"So, where's the rest of your family?" he asked between deliciously warm syrupy mouthfuls.

"Family?" Rhydian shook his head. "There's only me."

"What, no brothers or sisters?"

"Oh yes," said Rhydian.

"So where are they?" asked Tyler.

"Gone," said Rhydian matter-of-factly.

"Gone? What about your Mum and Dad?"

The Dragon shook his head sadly.[12]

"Oh, that's really sad," said Tyler.

Rhydian sighed. "Is it? I've never really given it much thought." The Dragon paused. "That's just the way it is."

"Suppose so," said Tyler munching his way through a roasted banana. "Still sad though." He took another bite of the yummy fruit. "Tell you what, I'll be your friend."

---

[11] Bronze Dragons are exceedingly rare and have only a very small entry in *Pong's Great Encyclopaedia of Dragonkind.* §

[12] Dragons have an uncanny ability of instinctively knowing their Dragon family tree in great detail. §

"My friend?" Rhydian took another loaded skewer, swallowing it in one hearty gulp. "I've never had a friend."

"Well, now you've got me," said Tyler. Suddenly, he had a dazzling thought. "Hey, we don't have to be friends."

"We don't?" said Rhydian, a little disappointed.

"No," replied Tyler, "you can think of me as your little brother!"

The Dragon paused deep in thought. "Why thank you, Master Tyler Bradley, but I really don't think it's possible for you to be my little brother."

Tyler stopped eating mid-bite.

"You're simply *too little,*" continued the Dragon. "How about you being my *Very Little Brother*?"

"Awesome!" grinned Tyler, unaware of all the fruity bits stuck in his teeth.

"Would you like something more to eat, Very Little Brother?"

"No thanks, I'm stuffed." Then a sudden horrible thought struck him. "Oh no, I'm in for it now! I've been gone too long. Dad's going to be breathing fire!"

"Wow! Just like a Dragon," said Rhydian clearly impressed by this new fact.

Tyler laughed. "No, he won't really breathe fire." The Dragon looked confused and slightly disappointed. "He'll be annoyed because he doesn't know where I am."

"Do you want me to have a word with him?"

"Yes… er… perhaps not," replied Tyler.

The Dragon nodded. "You will take some fruit with you, won't you?"

"Cool!" said Tyler.

"Cool enough by now, I should think," replied the Dragon.

Tyler laughed. "I'm going to enjoy having you as a big brother!"

"*A very BIG Brother!*" boomed the Dragon laughing at his own joke and sending wreaths of blue fire spiralling upwards.

Tyler took some fruit off the skewer and said his farewells. Half way down the tunnel, he heard a booming voice.

"Do come back soon, little Tyler!"

"Don't worry, I will," Tyler shouted back. "Hey, Rhydian, how old are you?"

"How old?" came the reply. "Never really thought about age. Is it important?"

"I think it's important for brothers to know each other's ages. I'm nine."

"Nine what?" asked Rhydian.

"Nine years old, silly," snorted Tyler. This was the second time he'd called a Dragon 'silly' – not many older brothers would be happy at younger brothers calling them 'silly' all the time. Tyler hoped this wasn't the case with older Dragon brothers.

"Nine years old, eh," mused Rhydian. "I guess I must be over forty."

"Forty? That *is* old. You're about the same age as my Dad."

"Your Dad is forty thousand years old? Do you think he might have known my parents?"

Tyler laughed. "Not forty thousand, just forty. My Dad's about forty years old," he was about to add the word, 'silly', but thought better of it.

"Forty years old? Why, he's barely older than an egg!"

The Dragon exploded with laughter. Fortunately, Tyler had grabbed his coat and scarf and pushed himself through the secret exit seconds before blue fire and smoke filled both the cave and the tunnel behind him.

Deep inside the secret cave, the huge Dragon finally managed to stop laughing. Curling up next to the barbecue, he settled down to sleep, chuckling to himself. "Fancy that, a Very Little Brother..."

Meanwhile, outside Tyler's snowman regarded him blankly as Dad walked across the Mountain towards him, unaware of his absence. Relief turned to horror when Tyler realised he was still carrying armfuls of freshly barbecued warm fruit.

How was he going to explain this?

He dumped the fruit next to the half banana still sticking out of the mountainside before hastily covering the fruity pile with snow, providing an extra marker to the secret

entrance. Fortunately, the fruit was no longer hot enough to melt the fresh covering of snow.

The chilled air prompted Tyler to put his coat back on as he walked over to the snowman. "Not a word, Snowy!"

The snowman stared blankly ahead and said nothing.

Tyler's Dad regarded his son sternly. "I know what you've been up to, Tyler Bradley."

Tyler froze - had his Dad seen him exiting the Mountain after all?

"Dad, I can explain—"

His Dad smiled. "You've been building a rather splendid snowman!"

Tyler sighed a huge sigh of relief.

"I know," said his Dad, excitedly. "Let's build another one. Here's a nice mound of snow." Dad stepped towards the hidden fruity mound.

"No!" cried Tyler. "Er... let's go home, I'm starving."

"Good idea," said his Dad. "I'm sure we've both had enough excitement for one day."

"You bet," Tyler doubted if anything could be as exciting as discovering a Dragon living deep within Rudry Mountain!

Chapter Five

A VISIT TO GRANDPA'S

They had some lunch, although Tyler couldn't eat much – his stomach was full of barbecued fruit and his head crammed full with thoughts of his new Dragon brother.

His Dad eyed him suspiciously. "I thought you said you were hungry?"

Fortunately, before Tyler could come up with an excuse, Mum came to his rescue, announcing she was leaving to visit Grandpa.

"Great, I'll come!" said Tyler, springing to his feet.

Twenty minutes later, he was sitting in Grandpa's living room warming in front of a blazing fire while Mum pottered around upstairs.

"I found the secret!" Tyler said in a loud whisper.

Grandpa stood by the fireplace, his gaze, lost in the flames of the fire. "Secret?"

"You know, the Mountain - there's no snow on it!"

Grandpa glanced out the window. "Happens every time," he turned to stare back into the flames. "It's a funny thing, fire."

Tyler's heart was in his mouth. "You know about the fire?"

"Oh yes," mused Grandpa. "The flames are alive, taking on all sorts of weird and wonderful shapes, you know."

"What about Dragons?" asked Tyler, the question tumbling out of his mouth before he could stop it.

Grandpa's head snapped round. *"Dragons?* What do you know about Dragons?*"

Tyler reeled. "Nothing - I was hoping you could tell me something about them."

"Dragons," sighed Grandpa, his gaze once more lost in the flickering flames. "Nothing but trouble... breathing fire, here, there and everywhere." Grandpa stoked the hot coals. "Some say they don't exist," he turned flames dancing in his eyes, "but I know better."

"You do?" Tyler could barely contain his excitement.

"Yup," Grandpa's face darkened. "I've seen one."

"You have?" Tyler's jaw dropped.

Grandpa leant in close. "Can you keep a secret?"

Tyler nodded, his mouth still hanging open.

Grandpa glanced around the room to check that they were still alone. When he spoke again, his voice was low. "Okay, I'll tell you. Many years ago, when I was courting your Grandma, we would go out sometimes spending entire evenings dancing beneath the stars; your Grandma was a great dancer!" Grandpa's gaze became lost as distant memories unfolded. "One night, just after seeing her home, I was looking up at the stars. It was a fantastic night with a New Moon. You know what a New Moon is, don't you, lad? It's where the sky is like the blackest of seas scattered all over with countless stars. You don't see it so much now, what with all these pesky street lamps blotting everything out, but back then, things were different, we had proper dark." Grandpa lifted his head, as if trying to look through the ceiling. "So, there I was, staring at the stars, marvelling at how beautiful they were, when suddenly, I saw it. It was barely visible against the black of the night, but I saw it, blacker than black." Grandpa's eyes were as wide as saucers. "At first, I thought it must be an aeroplane, but these wings were moving, like a giant bird. But I knew this weren't no bird." Grandpa bent in close. "Birds don't breathe fire!"

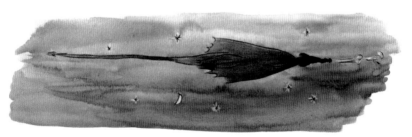

Tyler's heart was pounding. "What did you do, Gramps?"

"I ran. I ran and hid under a tree, huddling beneath the leaves, I was, shaking like a big leaf myself, thanking my lucky stars, he hadn't seen me!"

"You knew it was a 'he', then?"

Grandpa shrugged. "Well, I sort of assumed, and I certainly wasn't about to step out and ask - I mean, what do you ask a Dragon?"

A few suggestions sprang to Tyler's mind, but he kept his mouth shut.

Grandpa continued. "My heart was beating so fast and so hard, I feared the Dragon might hear it and eat me alive!"

"I know what you mean," nodded Tyler, his words escaping before he could stop them.

"Do you?" Grandpa's eyebrows arched in surprise.

Tyler shook his head. "Did you tell anyone, Gramps?"

"*Tell anyone?* What could I say? Who'd believe me? They'd most probably lock me up! But I know what I saw, and it was *real*. Very, *very* real."

"I believe you, Gramps."

Grandpa smiled and winked. "Good lad, now let's keep it our little secret," he said, tapping the side of his nose.

Tyler wondered whether he should tell his Gramps about his Dragon encounters too, but instead he decided to ask another question. "Have you seen any more Dragons?"

Grandpa shook his head. "Not sure I'd want to. Seeing one's more than enough for anyone."

Tyler's heart sank.

What if there were no more Dragons?

"Cup of tea, anyone?" Mum entered the room carrying a tray. "I've bought some nice fresh bread."

Grandpa's eyes lit up. "Time to put this fire to good use. Who'd like some toast done the old-fashioned way?" Grandpa's fireside toast was legendary. Picking up the long toasting fork always resident by the side of the fireplace, he pierced a slice of bread on its two large prongs (which Tyler thought looked something like a Dragon tongue), and held the fork at arm's length just in front of the flames. In a matter of seconds, the bread was browned and perfectly toasted. The delicious aroma made Tyler's mouth water. Grandpa flipped the bread over and toasted the other side. Soon they were all tucking in.

Grandpa smiled. "You can't beat scrummy fire-cooked toast!"

"You should try some barbecued pineapple," munched Tyler.

All eyes turned towards him. "I mean, wouldn't it be great to barbecue some pineapple cooked on the fire... if we ever got the chance?"

"I didn't know you liked pineapple," quizzed Mum.

"Er..." Tyler's thoughts raced, unable to think of anything.

Mum turned to Grandpa. "What have you two been talking about?"

Grandpa suddenly looked like a scolded schoolboy. "*Me? Nothing!*"

Mum shook her head. "Nothing indeed!" She gathered up the tea tray. "Boys and their secrets! Tyler, put your coat on, it's time we headed home to see what mischief your father's up to."

They trudged homewards through the snow; Tyler deep in thought.

Did Grandpa really see a Dragon?

Could it have been Rhydian?

What if it was another Dragon, perhaps even one of Rhydian's long lost family?

Tyler spent the rest of the day surfing the internet finding out everything he could about Dragons.

Dragons were:

🐉 Mythical

🐉 Magical

🐉 Fire-breathing (or sometimes acid or ice-breathing)

🐉 Treasure-hoarders.

Oddly, no one really believed Dragons ever existed (except Tyler and perhaps his Gramps). Notoriously ferocious, Dragons would often pillage towns and villages, swooping down to eat humans or animals in a single gulp.

Tyler grinned. His big Dragon 'brother' would be appalled.

That night, Tyler dreamt of barbecuing toast with his Grandpa in a circle of Dragons breathing their magical Dragon Fire...

Chapter Six

LOST AND FOUND

The next morning, Tyler's Dad announced he was heading out to do some more investigations on the Mountain.

"Can I come, Dad? I want to build some more snow people to keep my snowman company."

"Great idea," said Mum. "I'll come along too. I haven't built a snowman in years!"

Tyler had to think fast. "Sorry, Mum, this is something I need to do myself," he said, adding in a firm voice, "on my own."

"Oh, come on, Tyler, let me help, I used to be good at—" she stopped on seeing the steely look on her son's face, then she laughed. "Okay, you two, off you go!"

Soon Tyler and his Dad were trudging through fresh snow in search of adventure, their footprints of yesterday wiped clean.

Tyler's heart sank.

What if he couldn't find the entrance again?

Up ahead the un-snowy Mountain loomed, its green grass defiant against the chilling cold. As they got closer Tyler could see his snowman, deformed and misshapen by the fresh covering of snow.

"Looks like you'll need to tidy him up a bit," said Dad. "I can give you a hand, if you like."

Tyler had his mind on other things. "Nah, I can manage."

Dad ruffled Tyler's woolly hat. "Okay, you stay here. I've got some investigating to do."

So have I, thought Tyler as he watched Dad march up the mountain.

Tyler was just about to start some investigations of his own when his Dad stopped and turned. "And don't you be getting up to any mischief, Tyler Bradley!"

Tyler pretended not to hear as he began to remove the excess snow from his snowman. As soon as Dad was out of sight, Tyler abandoned the snowman to search for the hidden fruit concealed somewhere under the fresh snow. Unfortunately, there was not even the slightest hint of where the hidden fruit might be.

How could he have been so stupid?

Tyler kicked at the snow in frustration.

Up flew a frozen piece of barbecued pineapple!

What luck!

Tyler cleared away the snow and there was the banana marking the secret entranceway. Bracing himself for his next adventure, Tyler pushed against the side of the Mountain.

The Mountain remained solid.

Tyler tried again.

Solid.

He examined the banana closely - *it was barbecued*.

With a sigh of relief he searched the fruit again, this time for an un-barbecued banana, until eventually, there it was. With another shove into the mountainside, the ground reassuringly gave way. A few more pushes and he was halfway into the secret entrance.

"Tyler!" Mum's voice pierced the winter air.

Tyler tumbled backwards. Scrambling to his feet, he hurriedly piled snow over the barbecued fruit, shaping it into a large snowball as his Mum arrived.

"Tyler Bradley, you really are naughty. How dare you!" Tyler started to explain, but Mum cut him short. "How dare you leave home without your scarf."

"Sorry, Mum, I must have forgot."

53

Mum tapped him on the head. "You'd forget your head if it wasn't screwed on!" she wrapped the scarf around his neck. "Now, where's that father of yours got to?"

"He's up the Mountain with his instruments."

Mum tutted. "Typical. He knows I don't like you being alone on this Mountain, you never know what might happen. Your Grandma would be furious." Mum looked suddenly as if she'd said something she shouldn't. There was a short silence. "What were you doing anyway?"

"Nothing," replied Tyler innocently.

Her blue eyes pierced the wintry air. "*Hmmm... if I didn't know better, I could've sworn you were trying to 'push' the Mountain."

"Push the Mountain?" Tyler laughed off the absurd statement. "I was just rolling snow to make another snowman." He pointed to the large snowball encasing the secret fruit.

"Why don't I give you a hand?" Mum took a step towards the snowball.

"No!" Mum stopped dead in her tracks. "It's all right, I can manage."

Tyler's Mum gave him a curious look and shook her head. "Okay, I'll leave you to it. Now don't go getting yourself lost, and be careful. The last thing I need is for you or your father to go missing!" Mum scanned the Mountain as if looking for something unseen. "I expect you both back in a couple of hours, or else I'll come out and find you and there'll be no lunch!"

"Will do," Tyler continued to make his snow family until Mum was out of sight. Then, checking all was clear, he pushed his way back through the Mountain's secret entrance into the Dragon's lair.

Chapter Seven

JEWELS, POO AND ADVENTURES

The inside of the Mountain seemed incredibly dark after the brilliant white of the snow outside. Tyler's eyes adjusted quickly and after a few moments he could see the tunnel ahead leading to the cavern entrance. As he walked, the aroma of fruit got stronger and stronger. Tyler's excitement grew as his pace quickened.

"Hello, Very Little Brother!" Rhydian's voice boomed down the tunnel, nearly knocking him off balance.

"You can see me?"

"Of course I can see you. I've been waiting for you all morning for breakfast! I've barbecued some fruit especially for you, although it might be a bit cold by now."

"Cold's fine," said Tyler, entering the cavern.

Some small skewers of fruit were arranged on a large gold plate. "I can warm it up for you, if you like?"

"Nah, don't bother," Tyler picked up the platter, his face reflected in the golden mirror. He remembered reading about Dragons and their Treasure. "This is a nice plate," he remarked.

"I don't normally use them," said Rhydian, "Come to think of it, I've never used them."

"Where did you get it?" asked Tyler.

"From there," Rhydian indicated another passage entrance at the back of the cavern before tucking into his barbecued breakfast.

"That's strange," said Tyler.

"What?" replied the Dragon.

"I don't remember that being there yesterday."

"It wasn't," munched Rhydian, "in a manner of speaking."

"What do you mean?"

"It was hidden," Rhydian chomped on another fully loaded skewer of fruit. "I hid it using Dragon Magic."

Tyler's eyes grew wide. "You can do magic?"

Rhydian nodded. "All Dragons can. It's the same Magic that hides the entrance to this cave."

"Oh, I see," said Tyler, beginning to understand.

"I hope you don't," said Rhydian, looking worried. "Otherwise we'll have everyone walking in here at all hours. I'll never get any sleep."

"Can I take a look?" asked Tyler.

"Sure, go ahead," replied the Dragon, pointing the way with a flick of his enormous tail.

Tyler ambled over to the passage which was filled with light. Not the blue-green-purpley light of the cave. This was a gleaming light reflected from masses of gold, silver and heaps of diamonds, sapphires, emeralds, rubies and other countless precious stones.

"Wow!" breathed Tyler. "Where did you get all this?"

"That stuff? It's always been there," said the Dragon dismissively, devouring more steaming fruit in giant mouthfuls. "Just never had an occasion to use any of it before."

"It's amazing!"

"You think so?"

"Yeah, it must be worth a fortune!"

"You humans are strange creatures," chortled Rhydian. "They're just bits of shiny metal and a few sparkly stones."

"They're more than a few bits and most probably worth loads and loads."

"Loads and loads of what?" enquired the Dragon, pausing mid-munch.

"Money," replied Tyler.

"Money? Is that something you eat?"

"No, but you can—"

"Much rather a piece of fruit myself," snorted the Dragon in disgust. "As I said, you humans are strange creatures."

Tyler waded through the piles of treasure. "Hey, there's something else here, really big lumps of goldie-brown stuff. Wow, there's a huge hole filled with piles of it."

"DON'T TOUCH!" warned Rhydian.

Tyler snapped his hand back. "Why, is it valuable?"

"No," replied the Dragon.

"I won't break it, I promise."

"You'd be sorry if you did," said the Dragon.

"I thought you said it wasn't valuable?"

"It isn't."

"So why can't I touch it then?"

"I didn't think you'd want to, I certainly wouldn't – it's poo."

"Poo?"

"My poo," said Rhydian, a little embarrassed, "that's my toilet."[13]

hard shiny layer

smelly Dragon poo
trapped inside

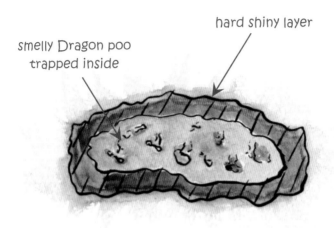

"Oh," said Tyler, making a hasty retreat to rejoin his big brother back in the main cavern. "So how did you get it?"

Rhydian stared quizzically in surprise. "*Get it?* You don't get it – it's poo – you get rid of it!"

---

[13] Dragon poo does not smell, at least not on the outside (on the inside it's very smelly indeed). This is because on exiting the Dragon (so to speak), Dragon poo oxides very quickly to form a hard shiny layer, while on the inside the incredibly smelly pooey stuff slowly degrades over time. Dragon poo comes in several shades and colours, often reflecting the colour of the poo-ing Dragon. Ancient Dragon poo has often been mistaken for something more valuable, something to be kept and treasured, although why anyone should want to collect very old poo is beyond any sensible Dragon.

"Not the poo," laughed Tyler, "the Treasure."

"Dunno," replied the Dragon. "It's always been there."

"Someone must've put it there."

"Doesn't matter anyway, what *does* matter is that your fruit is getting cold."

Tyler grinned, Rhydian was beginning to sound like his Mum.

"Maybe it was your Mum and Dad who left it."

Rhydian shrugged as he took some more fruit from the barbecue. "There's just me."

"But you said they were gone."

"They are, all the Dragons are gone."

"But, don't you think that's a bit *odd*?"

"*Odd?*" the Dragon paused to give this some thought.

"That they've gone."

Another shrug. "There's just me, I'm afraid."

"How do you know?" probed Tyler.

"I just do," replied the Dragon.

"I don't suppose you know where they've gone?"

Rhydian shook his head.

"Oh," said Tyler, not really knowing what else to say.

How terrible it must be to be the only one of your kind in the world, with no family, no friends, or no anyone. Tyler glanced over at the Dragon and guessed that he was thinking the same unthinkable thoughts too.

"Still, you've got me now, your Very Little Brother!" he said, trying to sound cheerful. "Hey, let's have some more fruit!"

"Fruit… yes… help yourself…" Rhydian was deep in thought. "Do you think we could go and find my family?"

"Suppose so," said Tyler, "but where do you start looking for Dragons?"

"Good question, how did you find me?"

"There was some fruit sticking out of the side of the Mountain," replied Tyler.

"Was there? Dear me, how careless! Who knows who might've wandered in? What were you doing on the Mountain anyway?"

"Well, my Gramps said that the Mountain had a—" Tyler stopped, quickly changing tack. "It was snowing and me and my Dad decided to go tobogganing, but when we got here there was no snow anywhere on the mountain and—" A thought struck him like a thunderbolt. *"That's it!* There was no snow on the Mountain!"

"Yes, I know," said Rhydian. "That's what you just said."

"But that's it, don't you see?"

"See what? There's nothing to see, and I, Very Little Brother, have *excellent* eyesight."

"There's no snow on this Mountain because you're living here. So, if *your Mountain* has no snow on it, then *other Dragon mountains* will also be snowless!"

The Dragon's eyes grew larger and larger. Then, he jumped high in the air, landing with an enormous

The whole cavern shook, sending treasure, fruit and Tyler tumbling to the ground. "My family, my family, we're going to find my family!" The huge Dragon skipped like a spring lamb.

Tyler scrambled to his feet, brushing bits of squashed fruit from his clothes. "*We?* Rhydian, I don't know…"

The Dragon stopped dancing, fixing the youngster with enormous hope-filled eyes. "You will be coming with me, won't you, Very Little Brother?"

Tyler's hesitation evaporated. "Yeah, sure, we're brothers, aren't we? But what are we going to do about my parents? They're not going to like me going off with a strange Dragon to look for lots of other lost Dragons."

"Oh," sighed Rhydian.

The cavern fell silent apart from the crackling of the huge bonfire.

"Unless we go at night," said the Dragon.

"At night?" said Tyler. "I can't."

"Why not?"

"Because it's night."

"And?"

"I just can't."

"Well, we certainly can't go by day. It wouldn't be safe, at least not for me," said Rhydian.

More silence.

"Then we'll have to go after everyone is asleep," announced the Dragon.

"But then I'll be asleep too," said Tyler.

"Don't worry," smirked Rhydian. "I'll come and wake you."

"Yeah, great," sighed Tyler. "You'll just knock on my door and ask my parents if we can go on a midnight Dragon hunt, right?"

"Not quite," said Rhydian, with a mischievous glint in his eyes. "But midnight, most definitely. I'll just use a little Dragon Magic."

"What kind of magic?"

"Just some Sleep Magic," said Rhydian. "One to keep your parents asleep while we're out searching, and to keep you, my Very Little Brother, awake."

"But we're not going to get very far in one night, especially walking in this snow."

"Who said anything about *walking*? We're not going to *walk,* we're going to fly."

"Fly?" exclaimed Tyler.

"Unless you'd prefer not to."

"I'd love to!" Tyler could hardly wait, he was going to fly on a Dragon!

They made plans to leave that very night at the stroke of midnight when everyone else was fast asleep. Rhydian said he'd bring some hot fruit for them to eat on their night adventure. With their plan in place, Tyler made his way back to the secret entrance. Once outside the Mountain, he continued making his snow family, barely able to concentrate.

Dad returned a short time later even more excited than the day before. Apparently, there had been a number of minor earthquakes while he was carrying out his experiments on the un-snowy Mountain. Dad asked Tyler if he'd felt anything. Tyler said he'd felt nothing at all, and that surely any tremors would have demolished his snow family. He had to stop himself laughing at the expression on his Dad's face – these unexplained 'earthquakes' being caused by Rhydian's jumping up and down!

When they got home, Tyler definitely didn't feel like laughing, especially when Mum asked him about all the fruit stains on his clothes. He managed to come up with some lame excuse about slipping on the snow, which stopped his Mum's questions, although she was far from convinced by his explanation.

Chapter Eight

GOOD SECRETS, BAD SECRETS

With more snow forecast, Mum and Tyler made another quick visit to Grandpa's with supplies of biscuits, cakes and a few other essentials.

Grandpa as usual was sitting in his chair, stoking the fire.

"I hear you've been up that Mountain again."

Tyler nodded. "Dad was doing some experimenting. He thought he felt some earthquakes."

"And what were *you* doing?"

Tyler was taken aback by his Grandpa's tone. "I was... er... building a snowman."

"Were you indeed?" replied Grandpa, prodding the hot coals with a poker as he stared into the flames. "That Mountain's got far too many secrets for my liking!"

"I suppose it is a bit strange," agreed Tyler.

"There's good secrets and there's bad secrets," stated Grandpa. "Wouldn't you agree?"

"I suppose so," Tyler shifted uneasily in his chair.

"Some secrets shouldn't be secrets at all, especially dangerous ones."

Tyler gulped.

"Dangerous secrets sometimes need to be shared." Grandpa paused, the ticking of the clock marking the silence. "You haven't seen anything up on that Mountain, have you, lad?"

"There's not a lot of snow," answered Tyler weakly.

"And have you ever wondered why that is?"

Tyler tried to sound casual. "I think that's what Dad's investigating."

"I wasn't asking your Dad, Tyler Bradley, I was asking you. Have you ever wondered why there's no snow up on that Mountain?"

"I-I'm sure there must be some explanation," Tyler's heart thundered beneath Grandpa's probing eyes.

"Good and bad secrets, lad, it's important to know which is which."

The door swung open. "Here's you tea, Dad, and some of your favourite biscuits." Mum set down the tray, but Tyler didn't feel like eating. "Now, what have you two boys been talking about?"

"The importance of secrets," said Grandpa, "and knowing when to tell."

"Secrets eh? Well, I'm sure you two have more than your fair share between you. Would you like me to leave you alone for some secret sharing?"

"No!" bleated Tyler.

"Yes," grunted Grandpa, both their answers colliding in mid-air.

Mum smiled. "I'd best leave you to it then. I've got a few more things to sort out before we leave."

As the door closed behind her, Tyler knew he had to say something.

"Gramps, would you do anything to help a friend?"

"Depends," replied Grandpa, "on what the 'anything' was."

"Well, if they needed to find something; something valuable."

"We've all lost something valuable, lad, at some time or another."

"Part of your family," continued Tyler.

His words hit Grandpa like a thump in the stomach. "Family's the most important thing of all, lad. Finding someone who's lost is not always easy, sometimes it's impossible."

"Impossible or not, if you could help them, you would, wouldn't you?"

Grandpa sighed as he slumped back in his chair, eyes lost in the flames. "Yes, I would, lad. Yes I would."

"And if you couldn't tell anyone else, even if you wanted to because you really wanted to help your friend so badly,

69

would that be a good secret or a bad secret?"

Grandpa turned, his eyes sad. "That'd be a good secret, lad. One well worth keeping." Grandpa smiled as he leant forward. "Now, are you sure you don't want one of these biscuits?"

Tyler spent the rest of the day secretly gathering together his night exploration equipment consisting of the following:

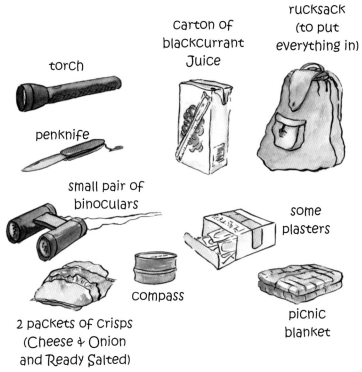

rucksack
(to put
everything in)

carton of
blackcurrant
Juice

torch

penknife

small pair of
binoculars

some
plasters

compass

picnic
blanket

2 packets of crisps
(Cheese & Onion
and Ready Salted)

Stashing the secret supplies into his rucksack, he stowed it out of sight under his bed. At eight o'clock he changed into his pyjamas and announced that he was off to bed. Once inside his bedroom, he stripped off his pyjamas and re-dressed in warm winter clothing. Then, climbing into bed fully dressed, he waited for his adventure to begin.

He glanced over at the clock:

Tyler closed his eyes and tried to relax, but with every passing second he was getting warmer and warmer, and hotter and hotter until eventually he could take no more. Tyler threw off the bedclothes, bathed in sweat.

Tyler lay in the dark for ages and ages. He was just beginning to doze off when he heard a creak from outside in the hallway. Yanking the bedclothes, he covered himself just in time as his bedroom door slowly opened...

It was then that he realised he was still wearing his woolly hat! Snatching it under the sheets just in time, he pretended to be asleep. After long seconds, the bedroom door clicked shut again.

Minutes later, the whole house was cloaked in darkness.

A relieved Tyler threw back the bedclothes and glanced at the clock:

Not long now.

He pulled back the curtains, the Full Moon flooding his bedroom with the silvery light.

Would Rhydian be on time?

Would he even show up?

Can Dragons even tell the time?

How would Rhydian know when midnight was?

Then an even more worrying thought struck him: *How would Rhydian even find him?*

In all the excitement, Tyler had forgotten to tell Rhydian where he lived!

How could he have been so stupid?

All this worrying and the lateness of the hour proved far too exhausting and within a few minutes, Tyler was fast asleep.

Chapter Nine

CONFRONTATION!

Tyler woke with a start. He glanced at the clock.

Where was Rhyd—?

There was a tap on the window.

Tyler peered through the darkness towards the square portal of stars where a long Dragon tail drooped down, curling neatly under his window sill. Throwing off his bedclothes, Tyler scampered to open the window. The night air snapped and bit, jolting him fully awake.

"Climb on to my tail, Very Little Brother," said a voice from above, a little too loudly for Tyler's liking.

"SHHHH! You'll wake Mum and Dad!"

"Don't worry, Very Little Brother, an earthquake and six thunderstorms wouldn't disturb them, but hurry, the Dragon Magic won't last forever."

"Wait a moment," Tyler crept back to his bed, plumping up his pillows into a sleeping Tyler-like shape before covering them with bedclothes. Strapping on his rucksack, he clambered out on to the Dragon's tail, closing his bedroom window behind him.

"Hold tight, Very Little Brother," The tail lifted him up on to the roof where a Dragon silhouette gleamed silver-bronze in the moonlight. "Climb up on to my back, between my wings."

Tyler gasped at how big his Dragon brother was, not only as big as a double-decker bus, but maybe three or four times as long! Rhydian flexed his wings to their full span, the moonlight glittering off bronzed scales like silvery-gold diamonds.

"Are you all right, Very Little Brother?"

Tyler nodded, all his senses tingling as he sat astride the huge Dragon, its metallic scales toasty warm in the chill of the night. "How did you manage to get here bang on twelve o'clock?"

"Well," explained the Dragon, "I always know the time because I can read the stars to within a few seconds. But as this was a very important appointment that I didn't want to miss, I flew down to a place you humans call Loon Down where they have a big timepiece which always shows the correct time – Big Den, I think you call it."

"Big Ben," corrected Tyler, "it's in London."

"Big Ben, that's what I said." The Dragon looked a little concerned. "Was I late?"

"No, you were bang on time."

"Did I bang?" asked Rhydian, looking even more worried now. "I certainly didn't mean to—"

Tyler chuckled. "It's okay, you were as quiet as a mouse and right on time!"

The Dragon smiled, ferociously sharp teeth glistening in the moonlight. "A rather big mouse, I suppose, but I'm glad I was on time, I would have hated being late and keeping you waiting so I left the mountain early about fifteen minutes ago."

"You flew to London and back in fifteen minutes?" said Tyler in disbelief.

"I didn't want to rush," said the Dragon matter-of-factly.

"But how did you find my house? I forgot to tell you where I lived."

"I followed your smell."

"My smell? I don't smell. I had a good wash before going to bed."

Rhydian laughed. "Don't worry, Very Little Brother, *ALL humans* smell, and every one of them is unique."

"So, what do I smell of?"

"You smell of... Very Little Brother."

"Is that a good smell?"

"Why yes, it's an excellent smell."

"But what if I *didn't* smell?"

"*You do*."

"But what if I didn't, how would you have found me then?"

"Mmmm... I guess I would have followed your footprints."

"My footprints?"

"Yes, your footprints from the Mountain to your house."

"But surely they're gone by now?"

"Enough questions, Very Little Brother, or else it'll be dawn and the whole night will be wasted." The Dragon braced himself for take-off, "Hold tight now!"

"*Wait!* Weren't you supposed to bring the fruit?"

The Dragon groaned. "I knew there was something. I was so excited about our adventure that I completely forgot! Hold tight, we'll get some now."

Rhydian launched himself up into the midnight sky. Tyler's stomach twisted and sank right down into his boots as the farmhouse fell away beneath them. Seconds later, Rudry Mountain loomed. Without slowing, the Dragon was through the side of the Mountain and into the secret lair. Skidding to a stop by a pile of fruit, Rhydian took a long slow breath. The seat of Tyler's pants grew a little hotter. Then the Dragon breathed out and blue-green flame roasted the fruity pile in seconds.

"That should be enough to keep you warm for the journey as well as a nice tasty snack for me!" The fruit bobbed on wreaths of smoke before plonking down neatly behind Tyler. "Now, hold tight, it's time to go."

Tyler braced himself.

"WAIT!"

Both boy and Dragon froze.

A figure stepped out of the shadows.

"Gramps!" Tyler nearly tumbled off the Dragon's back.

"Get yourself down, lad. Me and this Dragon's got some unfinished business."

Tyler quickly dismounted and slid to the ground.

Rhydian said nothing, the Dragon captivated by what was in Grandpa's hand: Grandma's treasured walking stick.

"Recognise this, do you?" Grandpa shook the ornate carved stick vigorously.

The Dragon stared as if in a trance.

"And well you should. Now where is she?" Grandpa's face was boiling as he cracked the stick on the ground right under the Dragon's nose. *"WHERE IS SHE?"*

"Rhydian—?"

"It's okay, Very Little Brother," the Dragon swung his enormous head back towards Grandpa. "She's not here."

"She?" Tyler was confused.

"Your Grandmother," snapped Grandpa. "This Dragon's gone and taken your Grandmother!"

"But, Grandma's dea—"

"No, she may have been dying, but she was far from dead," snarled Grandpa. "Now what have you done with her?"

"Gramps, there must be some mistake—"

"There's no mistake," said Grandpa, his eyes never leaving the Dragon. "Ask him."

Tyler hesitated.

"Go on, ask him!"

"Rhydian..."

"It's true, Very Little Brother, I did take her."

Tyler's world somersaulted uncontrollably. " Grandma, is here?"

Rhydian shook his head. "She was, but she... vanished."

"What have you done with her?" demanded Grandpa.

"I did nothing. She just vanished."

Tyler's mind was in free-fall desperately trying to right itself. "I don't understand..."

"Your Grandpa's right, your Grandmother was here." The Dragon paused before continuing. "She was very ill when she found the secret entrance."

"But how—?"

"The walking stick," said Grandpa. "It reveals the entrance. I don't know how, but it does."

"My eggshell," said Rhydian. "That's my eggshell on the top. It can detect Dragon Magic."

Grandpa rubbed his hand over the bronze head of the walking stick. "Your Grandmother said it was an old fossil found by one of her distant ancestors and passed down through the generations."

"But you said she was dead."

"I know, lad, I know. It was the easiest explanation. The truth was, your Grandma was dying and there was no cure. I was determined to look after her, but she didn't want any fuss, wanting everything to carry on just as if there was nothing wrong. One day, we went out on the Mountain for a walk and she twisted her ankle. I went to get help, but when I came back, she was gone." Grandpa's voice wavered, his eyes began to fill with tears. "I couldn't tell you, lad. I had no explanations myself. The police were called but there was no sign of her anywhere. The only thing that was left was her walking stick which was found on the side of the Mountain."

"She walked in here," said the Dragon.

"But how, Grandpa said she'd hurt her ankle?"

The Dragon shrugged.

Grandpa groaned in realisation. "She was faking it, just to get rid of me."

"Your Grandmother was weak and very ill," said the Dragon. "I tried to take care of her, and for a time, she seemed to get stronger. Then, without warning she vanished." Rhydian shook his head in dismay.

"But you said I was the first person here. You lied. You lied to me!"

"I didn't lie... I forgot."

"How can you possibly forget and now suddenly remember?"

"I don't know how, Very Little Brother, but that's exactly what happened."

The Dragon was telling the truth.

"But how could she just vanish? Your eyesight's brilliant. She couldn't just vanish, she just couldn't. You're both lying, everyone's lying!"

Grandpa rested a hand on his shoulder. "I didn't know what else to do. I couldn't explain it myself, how could I possibly explain it to you?" Grandpa crouched, their eyes level. "Besides, I knew... I knew she wasn't dead. I felt it, deep inside, in here. I felt it then and I feel it now. She's alive, lad, I know it, all we got to do, is find her."

An unexpected silence filled the Dragon lair.

"There's only one thing left to do," said Rhydian. "We go looking for our missing families – yours and mine."

Grandpa nodded. "Something tells me these two disappearances are linked. What say we go and find out, together."

"But Gramps, aren't you a bit old to —?"

"Now you're beginning to sound like your mother, Tyler Bradley. I was riding wild ponies well before I was your age."

Grandpa looked the Dragon up and down. "This is the same, just a bit bigger, that's all."

Minutes later, they were ready to go, Tyler in front with Grandpa tucked in behind.

"Hold tight, you two – let's go and find our families!"

Chapter Ten

NIGHT JOURNEY NORTH

"**W**oo-hoo!" whooped Grandpa as they soared up into the diamond sky.

Tyler clung to the Dragon's back, the Moon close enough to touch. Full and bright in the sky, its face beamed its secret smile, dappling the ground with silver shadows. Distant cities and towns punctuated the landscape in pools of orangey light.

"Is everything all right back there, Very Little Brother?"

"It's amazing!" breathed Tyler, more alive than ever.

"It is rather nice isn't it?" agreed the Dragon. "Although I rarely fly when the Moon is out." Rhydian banked, seeking out invisible updrafts in the night air. "I do hope you're warm enough."

c"Toasty, thanks," replied Tyler, the cold more than cancelled out by the warmth radiating from his big brother's body.

"Do help yourself to some fruit if you're hungry," urged the Dragon. "Now, hold tight, we're going to climb a little higher."

With a few mighty wing-beats, Rhydian climbed higher into the night sky, the snowy landscape stretching like a magical white tablecloth.

Tyler sighed. There wasn't an un-snowy mountain anywhere to be seen.

Rhydian banked hard to the right. Tyler screamed as he lost his balance, toppling off the Dragon's back. Fortunately, Grandpa caught him just in time!

"Oops sorry!" apologised the Dragon. "I'm not used to carrying passengers and I forgot you were there for a moment." Rhydian's head scanned left and right. "I can't see anything in the South, so let's head North."

On and on they flew, Rhydian pointing out this star and that star, making particular reference to one of the long snaking constellations.

"That's Froo-Arggh, my Great Dragon Forefather."[14]

Tyler looked up. "Your Great Dragon Forefather lives in the sky?"

"In the stars themselves," replied Rhydian.

"Wow!" breathed Tyler.

---

[14] Froo-Arggh *is the shortened name for* FRRROGARR-GWRRRIOORR, the Great Dragon ancestor of all Dragons. §

Soon they were over the mountains of North Wales rising like towering snow giants as the orangey pools of light from cities and towns became far less frequent.

The North was even more beautiful than the South, the majestic mountains and gleaming landscape taking on a dreamlike quality. The only disappointment in all this wonder was that there was no sign of any un-snowy mountains anywhere.

Tyler's heart sank.

Maybe Rhydian was the only Dragon after all.

A deep Dragon sigh echoed Tyler's hidden thoughts.

"There's nothing here," groaned Rhydian.

"What about Snowdon?" suggested Tyler.

"They're all snowed on, Very Little Brother, that's the problem."

"Snowdon is the name of a mountain – it's the biggest one in Wales."

"Oh," sighed Rhydian.

"What's up?" asked Tyler.

"It's the opposite of my Mountain."

"But it's Snowdon, the biggest mountain in Wales; yours is bound to seem small."

The Dragon shook his head. "No, all these mountains are snowed on; mine is un-snowed on."

Tyler laughed. "So, maybe we should rename Rudry mountain Un-Snowdon mountain!"

"Un-Snowdon mountain, that's very funny, Very Little Brother!"

The Dragon roared as they soared through the night.

"Wait a minute," said Tyler, "that's it!"

"That's what?" asked Rhydian.

"Under Snowdon mountain, the biggest of all Welsh mountains - it's the obvious place for all the Dragons to hide away."

"It was one of Grandma's favourite places too," added Grandpa.

"You may well be right. Hold tight you two, we're going down."

Rhydian folded his wings and fell out of the night sky, plummeting earthwards. The ground loomed at impossible speed. Tyler wanted to scream but nothing came out.

Moments from crashing, the Dragon extended his wings, sweeping along the valley bottom, he zig-zagged in between the sleeping mountain giants. Grandpa and Tyler held on to each other, laughing ecstatically as they soared over darkened farmhouses, woodlands and streams. The rumble of fire echoed deep within the Dragon's belly as Rhydian let out a mighty roar, sending a blaze of blue-green-purpley fire high into the night sky.

So much for secrecy, thought Tyler.

They came to a sudden halt, hovering in mid-air before dropping down at the foot of the great mountain.

Chapter Eleven

DRAGON FIRE!

"**D**o you see it, Very Little Brother?"

Tyler peered into the darkness. "See what? Everything's covered in snow."

"You don't see *anything*?" enquired the Dragon, staring intently.

"What, that big mound of snow?"

"Yes."

"It's glowing," Grandpa slid off Rhydian's back, eyes locked on the large snowy embankment.

Tyler jumped off the Dragon's back to join his Grandpa.

"Here," Grandpa handed him Grandma's stick. "Now, look!"

The snow pile glowed with a faint aura.

"It's Dragon Magic," said Rhydian, "ancient Dragon Magic."

"Let's go take a look," said Grandpa, striding forward through the snow with Tyler trailing behind.

The Dragon didn't move, his headlamp eyes looking as if they were about to explode into tears.

"Come on, silly! There's nothing to be afraid of. We'll look after you."

After a moment's hesitation, the Dragon stepped forward, its huge talons sinking deep into the snow which crunched and hissed.

"This Dragon Magic has been undisturbed for many thousands of years. It's protecting something. Go and stand behind those rocks, and don't come back out until I tell you, no matter what happens."

Tyler didn't like the tone of what his Dragon brother was saying but was too afraid to argue as Grandpa ushered him away.

Rising up on his hind legs, Rhydian drew a deep breath. The air crackled as the Dragon breathed out. Blue-green-Dragon Fire engulfing the entire lower side of the mountain, evaporating the snow instantly in billows of steam as the grass underneath burned away. Still the flames came, *hotter* and **Hotter** and **HOTTER**; the earth and rock glowing *brighter* and *Brighter* and *BRIGHTER* in the intensity of the Dragon Fire. Tyler and his Grandpa were forced to look away as the side of the mountain blazed like a miniature sun, the Dragon now the faintest of silhouettes in the brightest of lights.

94

Even from the safety of their rocky hideaway, the snow around them began to melt in the searing heat. Tyler was beginning to wonder if they would be safe when

The mountain exploded around them, spraying debris and acrid smoke everywhere.

The night became deathly still.

Eyes and throats stung raw, the two cautiously peered over the top of their rocky sanctuary. An enormous hole was in the side of the mountain, still smouldering with Dragon Fire. Rhydian lay completely still, eyes closed.

Tyler broke cover and ran to his friend's aid. Plumes of smoke streamed from Rhydian's nostrils as his huge mouth hung open.

The great beast wasn't breathing.

Tyler had to do something, fast!

It came to him in a flash - the Kiss of Life!

But how do you give the Kiss of Life to a Dragon?

Kissing was definitely out and thumping Rhydian's chest would have no effect at all.

But *jumping* up and down on it might! Clambering up on to the Dragon's chest, Tyler began:

95

One, two, three…

JUMP… JUMP… JUMP…

One, two, three…

JUMP… JUMP… JUMP…

One, two, three…

JUMP… JUMP… JUMP…

Nothing.

"Come on, Rhydian, come on, come on!"

Tyler tried again.

One, two, three…

JUMP… JUMP… JUMP…

One, two, three…

JUMP… JUMP… JUMP…

One, two, three…

JUMP… JUMP… JUMP…

"It's no good, lad, there's nothing you can do. Come down."

Ignoring the old man, Tyler carried on.

One, two, three…

JUMP… JUMP… JUMP…

One, two, three…

JUMP… JUMP… JUMP…

One, two, three…

JUMP… JUMP… JUMP…

"Come on, breathe you stupid—"

The ground rumbled.

No, not the ground, the Dragon.

Eyes still closed, a snaking tongue whipped out to grab some of the charred fruit scattered all around from the still steaming grass. An exhausted Tyler slid back to the ground.

"You did it!" cheered Grandpa. "Well, done, lad, well done!"

Suddenly, Rhydian's meandering tongue wrapped around Tyler's ankle like a whip, pulling his feet from under him.

"*Whoa! Hey stop!* Rhydian, it's me!"

Tyler's protests counted for nothing as the Dragon tongue began to retract, dragging the hapless boy towards the huge gaping maw.

"Rhydian, stop please! It's me, you've got my leg!"

Grandpa tried to disentangle his grandson, but the tongue was too tight. Gripping Tyler's arm, Grandpa dug in his heels, hauling with all his might, but all to no effect; now both were being pulled Dragonwards!

Fierce yellowy-brown teeth loomed, the smell of rotting Dragon breath overwhelming as a squirming Tyler was relentlessly trawled towards his unyielding fate. Grandpa thrashed the Dragon tongue of Doom frantically with his stick.

Tyler screamed, his body drenched in sweat as he was wrenched over the Dragon teeth, their granite hardness tearing through his winter clothing.

He was done for!

Sopping wet in pools of Dragon saliva, and the sickening Dragon breath clogging his nostrils, Tyler screwed his eyes tight shut and waited to be chomped in half like a boy-sized pineapple.

Morbid thoughts clattered through his panicked mind.

Would he die here or a bit later, roasting in the Dragon's fire-furnace belly? He hunched himself up into a ball, waiting for the killer crunch...

Suddenly, the tongue released, maybe to make way for the giant killer teeth. Sensing his last chance to escape, Tyler slid-slod over the slobbery confines of the Dragon's mouth, and launched himself over the terrible teeth. He hit the ground breathless, but at least he was alive.

Clearing the disgustingly sticky Dragon dribble from his face, a blurred Grandpa materialised, still wrestling Grandma's walking stick wedged firmly in the Dragon's jaws, desperately trying to retrieve it. Rhydian's eyes snapped open. Completely unaware of recent events, he opened his giant maw, catapulting Grandpa backwards, his treasured stick still in hand.

Rhydian looked on in horror. "W-W-What happened?"

"You tried to eat my grandson, that's what!" Grandpa shook his stick in fury at the Dragon.

"I did?"

"Yes, you did! I've got a good mind to—"

"It's okay, Gramps, he didn't mean it, he thought I was a piece of fruit."

"*A piece of fruit?* He should get his flippin' eyes tested."

"His eyes were closed, Gramps, I don't think he realised what was happening."

"I'm sorry, Very Little Brother, I meant you no harm. One minute I was trying to unlock the mountain's magic and the next, I felt this tapping on my chest and I could hear you laughing."

"He was screaming, you nincompoop!" reprimanded Grandpa.

"Sorry, it felt like it was all a dream."

"A nightmare, more like," grinned Tyler, his body shaking as much from relief as from the damp and the cold.

"I'm glad you're all right, little Tyler, but look at you, you're soaking wet!"

"That's because he was in your big gob!"

"Let me see if I can help." The Dragon opened his mouth and took a deep breath.

Grandpa moved protectively in front Tyler. "Oh no you don't, you're not barbecuing my grandson!"

"It's okay, Gramps, I don't think that's what he's got in mind."

Grandpa glared at the Dragon.

"I was just going to dry him off."

Grandpa reluctantly stood aside. "As long as you don't try to fry him, that's all."

"Close your eyes, Very Little Brother."

An ocean of warm air cocooned his body. In a matter of seconds, Tyler was completely dry - not only that, his torn clothing was also repaired!

"Good as new," said the Dragon.

And so he was, although Grandpa was still huffing and puffing under his breath something about demented Dragons nearly eating his grandson.

Rhydian looked around at the remains of his precious fruit strewn everywhere. "Dear, oh dear, oh dear, what a mess!" Moving his long neck this way and that, he gave it a sudden twist. A loud **_CRICKETY-CRACK!_** sounded as Dragon vertebrae clicked themselves back into place.

Rhydian eyed the fruit hungrily. "Do you mind?"

"Go ahead," smirked Tyler, "they're much more tasty than me!"

Needing no second invitation, the Dragon hoovered up the scattered fruit, wolfing it down in seconds.

"Ah, that's better, just what I needed. Nothing like some roast pineapples and bananas to fill you up after some heavy fire-breathing – a bit more well done than I would have liked though!" The Dragon smackered his lips, still savouring the taste. "Now, time to get on with our exploring!" Rhydian marched towards the still smouldering hole in the side of the mountain. "Follow me," he said, "and stay close."

Chapter Twelve

THE ORB OF DARKNESS

The secret cave was still glowing as they entered the mountain. Inside, the cave walls glimmered with the same magical light found in Rhydian's cave back in South Wales. Tyler and Grandpa's view of what lay ahead was blocked by the Dragon's massive bulk until they entered the main cavern. If Rhydian's lair was big, this was beyond all imagination! Towering walls lined with row upon row of cave entrances rose up as far as the eye could see.

Dominating the centre of the massive chamber was a huge dark glass orb. Ten houses in diameter, it floated off the ground just above head height, resonating with a low sounding thrum that prickled the skin. Not only that, the orb shimmered with darkness, its surface punctuated by sparks of bright blue lightning radiating from its depths.

Grandpa let out a long whistle as he wandered around the cavern.

"Wait here," instructed the Dragon.

Rhydian took off, flitting into each of the caves at impossible speed. Within minutes he was back, hurtling straight at the floating orb of darkness, studying the mysterious sphere from every angle and direction, trying to unlock its murky secrets. Then, with a loud groan booming like thunder as it echoed around the cavern, Rhydian slumped unceremoniously to the ground.

"What's wrong?" asked Tyler.

"They're all here," Rhydian replied in a low voice.

"The Dragons?" said Tyler. "What, *all of them*?"

"Every single one."

"Wow, that's great!" Tyler stared at the Dragon's glum expression. "Isn't it?"

"It would be, if they were awake."

"Cheer up, we can wait for a bit. We haven't got to be home for hours yet."

"I'm afraid it's going to be more than 'a bit', Very Little Brother," said Rhydian, becoming increasingly miserable.

"No worries, I'm sure that we can sneak out and come back again tomorrow."

"It won't be any good," replied the Dragon sullenly.

"Next week then."

"Next week, next month, next year, makes no difference."

"Well, *when* then?"

The Dragon stared at the glass orb then back at Tyler again. "When this thing goes off. It's an alarm clock. The Dragons will only wake up when it goes off."

Tyler approached the giant orb for a closer look. Deep within its depths, a universe of tiny stars and galaxies floated in the Black.

"So, when's it going to go off?"

The Dragon thought for a moment. "Unless my calculations are wrong, about fifty-three thousand, seven hundred and eighty-one years, four months and sixteen days, at about six-thirty in the morning, give or take an hour or so. It's difficult to be precise."

"*That long?* Is there any chance we can set it off early?"

"I suppose we could, but I don't think that would be wise."

"Why not, don't Dragons like wake up calls?"

"They're not *just sleeping*, Very Little Brother, they're in a Deep Sleep that has been sealed using the strongest Dragon Magic imaginable. Trying to break the Magic Seal might not be a good idea."

"What do you mean?"

"Any mistake in breaking the Magic Seal would result in breaking the whole alarm clock," replied the Dragon.

"So?"

"If we break the alarm clock, the alarm will never go off." Rhydian fell silent.

"And the Dragons will never wake up," finished Tyler.

"Exactly."

"Not ever?"

"Not ever," confirmed the Dragon. "They will go on sleeping forever and ever."

Tyler patted his big brother. "I'm sorry, Rhydian, I really am."

The Dragon sighed. "That's okay, little Tyler."

"So what are we going to do?"

"Wait," said Rhydian simply.

"*Wait?* For *fifty thousand years*?"

"Fifty-three thousand—"

"But you can't wait that long!"

"Why not? I haven't got anything else to do. I'm all alone."

"No you're not!"

The Dragon stared at him.

"You've got me."

Rhydian's giant head slumped to the floor.

"You're my brother!" protested Tyler.

The Dragon turned away, his giant chin scraping along the ground.

Tyler stomped across until he was face to face with the Dragon again. "I'm your brother... and what's more, you're mine! You're *not alone*, you've got *me!*"

Big Dragon tears welled up, but then, rather surprisingly, the hint of a smile.

"Indeed I do, Very Little Brother, indeed I do!" Rhydian's voice boomed. "Shall we go back home and I'll come back again later?"

Tyler's face dropped.

"Much later!" Rhydian added.

Both brothers burst out laughing.

A loud rapping sounded from behind.

Grandpa was lashing out at the underneath the floating orb, hitting it with all his might using Grandma's walking stick. Angry blue sparks fizzled around the sinister surface, as the ominous thrumming increased.

"Gramps, stop! You'll break it!"

The whole cavern shook, bits of rock now tumbling from the walls.

"That's exactly what I'm trying to do!" retorted Grandpa. "She's in there!"

"Who?"

"Grandma, she's in there! She's in there!"

Tyler rushed to stop his exhausted Grandpa. "Gramps, please, you mustn't!"

Tears were streaming down Grandpa's face. "I must get her out."

Tyler peered into the globe. The galaxies of stars were dissolving within the Black. "I can't see her anywhere, Gramps, are you sure—?"

"I'm telling you I saw her! Don't you think that I'd know my own wife?" Grandpa cracked the ornate stick on the ground.

"She is part of the clock," said Rhydian.

"What?" Grandpa glared, fire blazing in his tear-filled eyes.

"She's part of the clock."

"She's also part of me, damn it!" Grandpa lashed out with renewed strength and vigour. Before the stick could strike its target, a tendril of smoke gripped it, yanking it free, the stick now floating in wisps of Dragon Magic, well out of reach of the old man's desperate grasp.

"You can't break it. It's the only thing that's keeping her alive."

"And what about me?" pleaded Grandpa. "What about my life?"

The deep thrumming increased to a crescendo.

Another sound took its place...

A sound never heard before...

A sound too Dangerous to be imagined...

Chapter Thirteen

SHADOW DRAGON

The great orb grew darker and darker, lightning fizzling all over its surface.

The Black inside was moving and changing, taking shape, growing bigger and bigger as it emerged from the depths.

Rhydian spread his wings. "I think you'd better take cover."

A sinister, terrifying roar resonated as the orb began to flex and stretch.

Something was trying to get out.

Tyler and Grandpa were transfixed like statues.

A fierce Dragon head, made of complete darkness exploded through the orb's surface and roared. Its mighty bone-tingling bellow echoed around the enormous chamber as bit by frightful bit, the Shadow Dragon broke free, the secret cavern quaking as rocks fell all around.

Rhydian was already moving. "On my back, now!"

Tyler tugged at his Grandpa.

"Quick, Gramps! Quick!"

The old man was spellbound. Tyler was tugged away and thrust on to Rhydian's back.

"Hold tight, Little Brother."

Rhydian was climbing rapidly.

"We've left Gramps!"

"I've got to get you to safety."

"No, no, go back! Go back!"

Still the Bronze Dragon climbed, countless rows of caves now blurred in a fast moving haze.

"Rhydian, stop! Please, please stop!" Tyler pounded the Dragon's scales until his fists hurt.

Far below, the Shadow Dragon was already banking steeply towards the tiny figure frozen beneath the orb. The beastly apparition roared, the most horrible roar imaginable, its giant maw looming open, eager to devour.

Tyler stared in horror as the Shadow Dragon closed in on the hapless old man.

In a frenzy of shadow, Grandpa was gone.

"Noooooooo!"

Rhydian levelled out, hovering next to a ledge. "Get off, Little Brother."

Tyler was sobbing, unable to move.

"Little Brother, I need you to wait here, where you'll be safe."

"I don't want to be safe, I want to be with my Gramps."

"Please, little Tyler, while there's still time."

The Shadow Dragon was already turning and climbing rapidly.

"Tyler, move! Now!"

Closer and closer, the Shadow Dragon loomed larger and larger, moving at impossible speed. The two smashed into each other, the Shadow Dragon a black cannonball ramming Rhydian towards the top of the cavern. Thrown clear by the mighty collision of the two leviathans, Tyler tumbled...

Down... Down... Down...

Debris fell as both Dragons impacted the top of the cavern with a thunderous, sickening crash. Still plunging groundwards, Tyler lost all sense of reality, the ground screaming up at him like a mighty hammer.

Suddenly, he was floating, tendrils of Dragon Magic lowering him safely to the ground.

Instinctively, Tyler sprinted for cover somehow managing to dodge the lethal rain of falling debris.

High above, a tumultuous ball of Bronze and Shadow-Black plummeted downwards, both Dragons clawing and biting ferociously in their fight for supremacy.

Faster...
Faster...
Faster...
Down... Down... Down...

Then in an instant, both were gone – swallowed by the pulsating Orb of Darkness, its surface flaring outwards in a sonic boom, draining all light from the cavern.

Blackness

Then, everything was back to as it was, the orb resuming its low thrum as if nothing had happened.

The emptiness reached down into Tyler - into his stomach, his arms, his legs, his fingertips, his toes and his heart, every inch of him filled with something he had never felt before.

Despair.

He was alone, completely alone. More alone than he'd ever been before in his life.

Grandpa and Rhydian were gone.

Tyler stepped out into the vast emptiness of the cavern.

The dark orb thrummed its monotonous thrumming.

Otherwise nothing.

Nothing and no one.

He was trapped.

The terrible weight of the mountain bore down on him in its entirety.

He was alone with no way of ever getting home.

Tyler walked numbly towards the hovering glass globe. He stood beneath it, standing where Grandpa had stood just minutes before. The Darkness of the sphere above him mirrored the Darkness within him as he stared with blank eyes, longing for the orb to crush him. The Darkness was complete. Stars and galaxies were absent, as were the blue sparks of light running around the outside of the giant sphere. Apart from the continual thrum, the orb might as well be dead.

Dead.

Everything was dead.

The Darkness.

Grandpa.

Rhydian.

Dead.

What was he to do now?

What could he do?

Dark moved within the Dark.

Tyler backed away, his stomach somersaulting, wanting to be anywhere else but—

Wait...

Not entirely Dark.

Copper dark.

Bronze dark.

Glowing bronze, getting *Larger* and *LARGER*...

A high-pitched noise, piercing *Louder* and *LOUDER*...

The hurtling bronze, *Closer* and *CLOSER*...

Tyler flung himself aside, hands clamped over his ears desperate to muffle the agonising sound. The surface of the orb exploded with a mighty roar, a chaos of bronze as Rhydian broke free from its confines. Soaring high in a long arc, the Dragon wasn't alone.

There on his back, nestled safely between his wings was a solitary figure.

"Gramps!" Tyler sprinted forward as the Dragon skidded awkwardly to a stop.

Tyler helped the old man down from the Dragon's back.

Grandpa managed a weak smile. "Thanks, lad."

Tyler hugged his Grandpa, tears streaming down his face. "I thought I'd lost you, Gramps."

Grandpa ruffled his grandson's hair. "I thought I was lost there for a bit too, Tyler lad."

Rhydian was rasping like a broken steam engine. Scars deep and shadow black, criss-crossed his body.

Rhydian smiled, wearily. "You're safe, Little Brother. I thought I'd lost you..." The Dragon was finding it increasingly difficult to breathe. "I didn't want... to lose you."

Tyler patted the Dragon's snout. "I thought I'd lost you too, but you saved me! Now we can all be together, as a family, you and me and—"

"No, Little Brother... the Darkness... is spreading... inside..."

"What does that mean?"

"It means... I'm dying... there is no newness..."

"No newness, I don't understand."

"The Darkness..."

Rhydian was losing consciousness.

Moment by moment, the Dragon's body was darkening in shadow, becoming completely devoid of warmth.

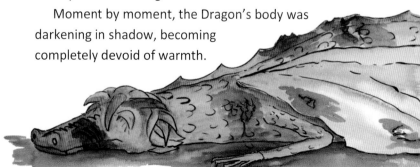

Grandpa took his arm. "Come on, Tyler lad, there's nothing we can do."

"But—"

"No buts, let him die in peace."

"But he can't die, he can't! He's my Dragon; he's my brother!"

Rhydian's breathing was becoming shallower and more infrequent as the insidious dark shadow crawled over his scales, slowly consuming the gleaming bronze.

"Wait! Grandma's walking stick!" Tyler scanned the debris-strewn floor for the missing cane.

"What about it?" asked Grandpa.

"We have to find it. It's our only hope of saving him."

"But—"

"It has newness."

"What?"

"Newness. It's Rhydian's eggshell on the top! Well, the eggshell is new!"

"Tyler lad, the eggshell's not new, it's a fossil thousands of years old."

"It may be old *now*, but it's where Rhydian came from when he was new – Ah, there it is!" Tyler rescued the cane from beneath a pile of dust and stones.

"So now what?" asked Grandpa.

Tyler's mind drew a blank, refusing to come up with any answers.

"Rhydian, I have your eggshell, from when you were born."

The Dragon lay motionless, the Shadow almost completely consuming his dying bulk.

"You can't die! I won't let you! I won't let you!" Tyler struck out with Grandma's stick, beating the shadowed scales over and over. "Stupid shadow! Stupid, stupid shadow!"

Sparks flew as fragments of ancient eggshell broke away, shattering against the hardness of the Dragon scales.

"Tyler lad, look!"

Tyler stopped.

Where the ancient eggshell came to rest on the scales, they started to liquefy, and where they liquefied, circles of shining Bronze appeared, chasing away the malevolent Black.

With his energy renewed, Tyler struck the Dragon all over in a rainbow of sparks. Wherever the ancient shell rested, a

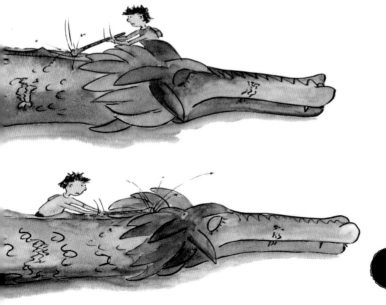

circle of restoration began, erasing the Black and restoring the Bronze!

When Tyler could no longer continue, Grandpa took over; then back to Tyler. Eventually there were no more sparks as ancient bronze shell gave way to wood.

Man and boy stood back, completely exhausted, Rhydian's scales a patina of Bronze circles surrounded by traces of Black, the Dragon resembling a huge Bronze-Black leopard.

Still the Dragon lay lifeless.

"Come on, Rhydian... come on, Big Brother," Tyler slumped against the Dragon's neck.

"There's smoke coming out!" said Grandpa.

The scales beneath Tyler's body started growing warmer.

"Rhydian?"

The giant Dragon head stirred. "I don't suppose we have any barbecued fruit left...?"

Before long, the Dragon was back to his shining bronze best, with just the slightest of traces of the malevolent Black running like scars across the scales. "I knew you could do it, my clever Very Little Brother!"

Tyler was overjoyed as his Grandpa sat slumped on the ground.

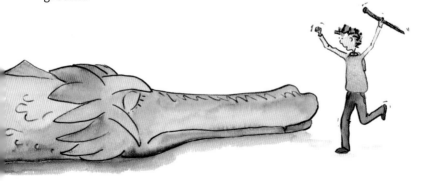

"You have your Dragon back, but what about my Muriel? Alive or not, she's lost forever inside that big thing and there's no way of ever getting her back."

Rhydian climbed to his feet. "There may be a way after all. Both of you, please stand back…"

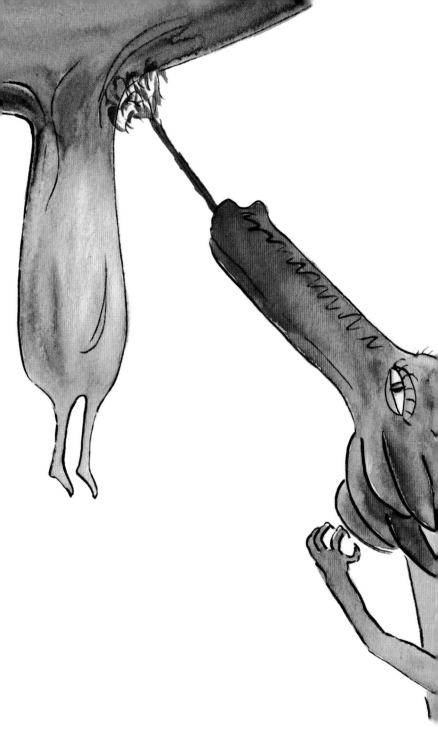

Chapter Fourteen

CHANCER ENCOUNTER

Facing the ominous Orb of Darkness, Rhydian took a deep breath. The Dragon's innards bubbled and popped and rumbled as the Dragon Magic brewed deep down inside. With eyes narrowed in deep concentration, the Dragon exhaled a thin fiery javelin spearing the Darkness of the orb. The impenetrable Black greedily swallowed up the fiery lance, but still the Dragon flame continued, a molten blob now appearing on the orb's surface. On and on the flame came, the blob glowing *Hotter* and *HOTTER*.

Hairs prickled on the back of Tyler's neck as he thought back to the Dragon Fire and its effect on the exploding snowy mound, and the dire consequences that followed for his Dragon brother.

Would this orb explode too? Or maybe the Shadow Dragon would be unleashed again and they'd be done for!

The blazing splodge shifted, beginning to separate from the underside of the dark sphere, slowly dripping downwards in a large molten globule. Still the Dragon flame continued, the blob now lengthening and changing shape, separating completely as it hit the ground. The flame stopped. Rhydian closed his eyes as the molten mass faded and cooled.

Tyler and Grandpa gaped open mouthed in disbelief.

Grandpa was already moving.

"MURIEL!"

Grandma smiled. "Reg dear, it's so good to see you again. I always knew that one day you'd find me!"

The couple embraced, grateful tears streaming down Grandpa's face.

"I knew you were alive, I knew it! I could feel you inside." Grandpa tenderly stroked his wife's hair. "You just vanished without a word."

"Reg dear, you sweet, sweet man, I was very sick, and although you did your best to put on a brave face, I could see it was breaking your heart."

Grandma smiled again, this time a sad smile as she caressed her husband's face. "I couldn't bear to see you so sad. I had to go away."

"But you didn't have to go—"

"I had to, Reg, before I became too weak and unable to do anything. That's when I thought that the Dragon might be able to help."

"You knew about the Dragon?"

"I know about a great many things, dearest."

"The stick—"

"The stick, yes, and a lot more besides," Grandma's gaze took in the vastness of the cavern. "So, I got the Dragon to bring me here, where I knew that I'd be safe."

"But he told us that you'd just vanished."

Grandma nodded. "Yes, dear, and as far as he was concerned, I did."

"But how—?"

"I have a little Magic[15] of my own."

"Magic—?"

Grandma put a finger to her husband's lips. "There's far too much to tell and far too little time, Reg dear." She glanced over towards Tyler.

---

[15] Tyler's Grandma was a Dragon Chancer. Sometimes called 'Chancers' and mostly females, they have Magic rooted deep inside, allowing them to sense, charm and control Dragons to do their bidding. With the disappearance of the Dragons, Chancers became obsolete and largely forgotten, and over time, even the Chancers themselves became completely unaware of their magical abilities.

"I see you've brought our little Giardd[16] with you! Come here, Giardd bach,[17] let me take a good look at you." Tyler stepped forward – only Grandma ever called him by his middle name. "My, my, just look at you, my fine young man!" Grandma stroked his cheek, her touch warm and full of memories.

"Oh, Grandma," Tyler flung his arms around her.

"There, there, Giardd bach, there's no need to break me!" Grandma crouched down, locking his gaze with hers. "Now, listen, I need you to do something for me. I need you to take your Gramps back home, it's where he belongs – *it's where you belong*. I must remain here, but don't worry, before you know it, we'll be back together again forever."

"But can't we—"

"You need to go home, Cariad bach,[18] you have a real live Dragon to look after!"

---

[16] Just like English names, many Welsh names have a deep and significant meaning, but *Giardd* (pronounced 'Gee-arth'), is unique with no apparent meaning at all.

[17] 'bach' (pronounced the same as the famous German composer, Johann Sebastian Bach), is a Welsh term of endearment meaning 'small'.

[18] Cariad is the Welsh word for Love.

"But Grandma, what about you? We can leave together."

"I belong to the Dragons, Cariad, I always have."

"But—"

"I'm part of their Magic, it keeps me alive, but it also binds and keeps me here, until a time where all is restored just as it was. Until then, part of me will always remain with you."

Tyler glanced over at his big Dragon brother, standing eyes closed like a statue.

"Don't worry, Cariad, he'll be all right. Look after each other and take good care of your Gramps." Grandma began to fade. "You're growing into a fine young man, Giardd. Now be off with you, I must go and so must you."

The dark orb crackled in the centre of the massive chamber.

"Come on," urged Rhydian, "I have to get you home before your parents wake up. Look, your Grandpa has already fallen asleep!"

Grandpa was asleep standing bolt upright and snoring loudly!

Something niggled at Tyler's memory...

Something wonderful...

Something missing...

Something...

"Come on, Very Little Brother, I would hate to be caught flying around after sunrise." The Dragon paused. "It's a shame though…"

"What is?" asked Tyler.

"Well, I really wanted you to meet my family and for them to meet my Very Little Brother."

"You found them then?"

"Oh yes, they're up in the—"

"Fantastic," said Tyler, "Can't we say a quick 'Hello' before we go!?"

Rhydian grinned. "Why yes, why not? What a splendid idea! Hop on to my back, Tyler, and hold tight!"

Clambering up and seating himself between the Dragon's wings, Tyler was soon joined by his sleeping Grandpa, wrapped in curls of Dragon Magic smoke, still snoring peacefully.

In a few wing-beats, they were spiralling higher and higher. Tyler hadn't noticed before, but the rows of caves on the bottom gradually decreased in size the higher they flew. Rhydian explained that the largest caves were for the Gold Dragons; the next smallest were for the Silver Dragons; then smaller again for the Blue and Black Dragons; and finally, the smallest caves were for the Red Dragons.

"Here we are," announced Rhydian, hovering outside a number of caves. "The Silver Dragons."

"But you're not silver?"

"I am," replied Rhydian, "at least in part."

Tyler was confused.

128

"My father is a Silver Dragon and my mother a Gold Dragon. I think that makes me quite unique and special."

"Most definitely," agreed Tyler, "you're very unique and special to me!"

"As you are to me, Very Little Brother, shall we go in?"

Tyler was nervous and excited all at the same time as they entered Rhydian's family cave.

"Very Little Brother," Rhydian announced grandly, "may I introduce you to the rest of my... I mean, the rest of *our* family."

And there, in the eerie Dragon light, Tyler was 'introduced' to Rhydian's parents and siblings, all magically frozen in stone like beautifully carved statues. Tyler couldn't be sure if all Dragons looked like their parents or their brothers or sisters, but in Rhydian's case, this was definitely true.

"They're beautiful, absolutely beautiful!" breathed Tyler awestruck. "I bet they miss you as much as you miss them, and I know that one day they will be very proud of you."

"Thank you, Very Little Brother," said Rhydian, "and I am proud of you too. Now, let us be going."

The three companions soared through the giant cavern, along the secret entranceway and back outside into the wintery weather.

Snow
was
falling...

Turning to face the mountain, Rhydian sang, his song a gentle roar both ferocious and beautiful causing the secret cavern entrance to glow brighter and brighter.

If Tyler could have understood the ancient Dragon tongue, this is what he would have heard:

Song of the Lost Dragons

When ice doth come in Winter's snow
Into Deep Sleep the Dragons go

The ice that comes is ice that goes
Into Deep Sleep the Dragons go

Encased in Stone that none may know
Into Deep Sleep the Dragons go

And when the Sun the ice shall melt
The Dragons will return
To rule the world with Stealth and Fire
The Dragons will return

From Deepest Sleep, the Deepest Sleep
The Dragons will return!

When the song was finished, the brightness of the lair entrance faded, once more cloaked and invisible by powerful Dragon Magic. Lifting his giant head, Rhydian breathed Dragon Fire high up the side of the mountain, causing an avalanche of snow to come tumbling down, completely covering the entrance to the secret Dragon lair.

"Now, Very Little Brother, it's time for us to go home."

And so home they flew, Tyler never wanting his Dragon adventure to end.

With his snoring Grandpa still aboard and Rhydian's assurances that he would drop Grandpa off safely, the Dragon deposited Tyler at his bedroom window just as dawn was breaking. Tyler gazed longingly as the Dragon vanished into the dawning light of a new day.

"There's something very strange about that Mountain," Grandpa said, "Have you ever wondered why the snow never settles?"

Tyler munched into his freshly fire-cooked toast but said nothing.

Grandpa stared out of the window at the Mountain, trying to uncover it's secrets. "Well, I'm sure your Dad will find something if there's anything to be found."

Tyler grinned silently to himself – he couldn't wait to see his Big Brother again!

Grandpa ruffled a calloused hand through his grandson's spiky mop of hair. "Well, that's enough of the Mountain secrets... Now, who's for some more fire-toast?"

Chapter Fifteen

THE OLD MAN ON THE MOUNTAIN

This was just the first of Tyler and Rhydian's many adventures together. There are more stories, but just for now, let me tell you a little of what happened to Tyler...

Humans age far more quickly than Dragons, and all too soon, Tyler was no longer a boy, but a young man. Distracted by other things, Tyler visited Rhydian far less often, until eventually, with the help of a little Dragon Magic, the young man forgot altogether.[19]

Tyler moved away to study at University, where he met and married a pretty young woman and together they had children of their own.

---

[19] Rhydian thought it wise for Tyler to go and live his life without any knowledge of Dragons, although he missed his Very Little Brother very, very much.

Only many years later did he eventually return to Rudry, home of the mysterious Mountain, but now as an old man with white hair, his wife having sadly passed away. With his children now grown up and living in different parts of the world, Tyler was alone.

The old man could often be seen walking around Rudry Mountain as if searching for something, carrying armfuls of fresh fruit and appearing to talk to the Mountain itself. Many of the local people simply thought he was a crazy old man, and many laughed at him behind his back.

One day, the old man was seen going out to the Mountain but this time he didn't return. The police were called but he was nowhere to be found. They did find something however – the man's battered old walking stick was discovered at the foot of the Mountain beside what appeared to be some barbecued fruit.

The following winter, when the snows came once more to the village of Rudry, something very strange and unusual happened. For the first time in thousands and thousands of years, the snow began to settle, covering the Mountain in a gleaming blanket of white!

Old Man Missing

An elderly man has gone missing from the small village of Rudry, in South Wales. Mr Tyler Bradley, aged 77, was reported missing by local villagers some three days ago.

Mr Bradley was last seen walking the countryside carrying several bags of fruit. On searching the area, police have reported finding an old walking stick, along with some charred fruit, although these have yet to be confirmed as those belonging to Mr Bradley.

It is not certain whether Mr Bradley has any surviving relatives, but it is thought that he was originally from the village. Mr Bradley has been described by locals as 'something of an outsider'.

Police have appealed for any relatives or friends to please come forward. At present, they are not looking for anyone else in connection with the disappearance, although the close knit community of Rudry have been advised to remain vigilant since the incident.

Rudry village and the surrounding area have become well known for the growing of exceptionally large fruit, but there is not thought to be any connection with this and the fruit found on the mountain.

Police are continuing with their enquires.

Dragon Appendix

A BRIEF HISTORY
OF
DRAGONS

Dragon Appendix

A BRIEF HISTORY OF DRAGONS

Long, long ago, when the world was a lot younger than it is today, there were lots and lots of weird and wonderful creatures that roamed the earth, many of which have since become extinct. By far the most wonderful and most *Magical* of all these creatures were the Dragons.

Now, Dragons were, by and large, very ferocious and horribly fierce, breathing out fire and smoke, and all manner of nasty things over everyone and everything. When hunting for food, they would soar high in the sky, and using their incredible eyesight they would spy their prey far, far below (see Dragon Note 1).

ഔൽ
Dragon Note 1

Dragons have exceptionally good eyesight, much, much sharper than any eagle's, who by comparison are considered to be as blind as bats!

For instance, a Dragon can count the freckles on your face from a distance of three miles!

Swooping down at high speeds, Dragons would often fry their helpless victims alive, even swallowing them in a single swooping gulp (larger Dragons were able to swallow sheep and cows whole).

Some of the more spiteful Dragons would scoop up their poor victims (without frying them with their nasty Dragon breath), and take them back to their lair to 'heat them up' later for supper. Other even meaner Dragons would just swoop down in a low arc and destroy everyone and everything in their path just for the fun of it (if indeed you can call that fun?).

Dragon Types & Kinds

Dragons come in all shapes, sizes and interesting colours (see Dragon Note 2).

ഇറ

Dragon Note 2

There are so many Dragons of varying shapes and sizes and colours, that it would be impossible to list them all here. One of the oldest and most highly regarded Dragons, the great Dragon Pong documented all the Dragon varieties in *'Pong's Great Encyclopaedia of DragonKind: Varieties, Types, Colours and Habitats'.*

Gold & Silver Dragons

The largest Dragons are the Gold and Silver Dragons (the Silver Dragons being not quite so big). These are the Royal Dragons and are very regal and majestic. Gold and Silver Dragons, unlike most other Dragons, are peaceful and not bad tempered or wicked at all.

Bronze Dragons

The offspring of Gold and Silver Dragons (who rarely cross breed), Bronze Dragons, are exceedingly rare (see Dragon Note 3).

Dragon Note 3

The rarest of all Dragons are the White Dragons which are perhaps the most beautiful (although other Dragons might dispute this fact). These majestically wonderful creatures are very private, keeping themselves to themselves. As such, very little is known about them, with scarcely a mention of White Dragons in *Pong's Great Encyclopaedia of Dragonkind: Varieties, Types, Colours and Habitats.*

Bronze Dragons are very good natured beasts, fortunately inheriting the very best traits of both regal parents.

Blue & Black Dragons

Blue and Black Dragons are notoriously bad tempered. Blue Dragons breathe shards of ice rather than traditional Dragon Fire, whereas Black Dragons can spray acid as well as scorching fire, which is not very nice at all.

Red Dragons

By far the meanest, wickedest and most horriblest of all Dragons are undoubtedly the Red Dragons. With the curious exception of the nature-loving Green Dragons (see Dragon Note 4), they are the smallest of all Dragonkind.

ஐ☙
Dragon Note 4

Green Dragons couldn't bear to leave their beloved forests, so they used their Dragon Magic to shrink themselves, preferring to hide away deep inside the forests and trees until the Ice Age had passed.

When the warmer temperatures finally returned, the Green Dragons rather liked being small and unnoticed, and so decided to abandon their Dragon Magic to become like normal creatures, which still inhabit some forests even today!

what the Red Dragons lack in size, they more than make up for with extra meanness and spitefulness (see Dragon Note 5).

More often than not, it is the Red Dragons who are likely to cause destruction and mayhem just for the fun of it (although Blue and Black Dragons are not that much better).

⸙⸙⸙
Dragon Note 5

Red Dragons are the meanest Dragons you could ever imagine. On a scale of 1 to 10, where 1 is an incy-wincy, tiny-weeny bit mean, and 10 is very, very, very, very, VERY mean), Red Dragons score at least a 15 !

Dragons & Wales

D ragons made their homes in many parts of the world, but they had a particular fondness for one place in particular, where they could be found in great abundance.

That place is called *Wales*

There is something very special about the Welsh mountains and hills that attract Dragonkind in the same way that bees are attracted to bright and beautiful flowers. That 'special something' is the intoxicating combination of the singing grass found on the Welsh mountains and hills, and the delicious water flowing through its valleys.

As well as possessing amazing eyesight, Dragons also have an acute sense of hearing (see Dragon Note 6). If you sit quietly on a mountainside in Wales and listen very carefully, there is a good chance that you will hear nothing at all, but this doesn't mean that there's nothing to be heard. When the wind blows off the sea from the West and sweeps across the Welsh mountains and hills, the grass gently sways, and it is this swaying, combined with the moisture in the air that causes the grass to 'sing' in the breeze.

৪০০৪
Dragon Note 6

Dragons can hear the quiet breathing of a sleeping dormouse from a distance of well over two miles!

This 'singing grass' is found nowhere else on earth, and it is this song that so enchants and draws Dragons from all over the world.

In addition, the valleys of Wales are teeming with clear rivers of delicious fresh water. In order for Dragons to make consistently good quality fire, they need the purest water available, and to the discerning Dragon, the water of Wales is like fine wine. It is this purity that makes for good fire-breathing (or acid-breathing, or ice-breathing - depending on the Dragon type).

Another reason that Dragons are drawn to Wales is the rich abundance of coal hidden deep within its mountains and hills. It is a well known fact that Wales has the finest quality coal to be found anywhere on Earth - just ask any Dragon, or failing that, the driver of any steam train (see Steam Train Note 1).

ℰℂℜ
Steam Train Note 1

In the so called 'Golden Age of Steam' high quality coal from Wales was exported to power steam trains all over the world.

All Dragons (except the Blue ice-breathing Dragons) love nothing more than snuggling down deep in the heart of a mountain surrounded by hot glowing coal. Coal found in Welsh mountains stays toasty warm for days on end.

One final reason why Wales was so popular with all Dragonkind is the abundance of sheep. There are thousands and thousands and thousands of sheep to be found grazing on its mountains and hills - in fact, there are more sheep in Wales than there are people! Dragons love eating Welsh sheep even more than eating humans! Dragons can't get enough of them, gorging on sheep day after day (see Welsh Lamb Note 1).

ഇൻ‌ൻ
Welsh Lamb Note 1

Welsh Lamb is really tender because they are continually feeding on the lush singing grass and drinking the pure Valleys water.

Dragons would regularly fly in from all over the world to feast on Welsh Lamb, whilst sitting on the mountainsides listening to an impromptu concert from the singing grass under the stars!

So, it is because of the singing grass, pure water, rich coal and an abundance of quality sheep that many Dragons decided to make their homes deep inside the mountains of Wales.

It is no coincidence that the Welsh flag has a Dragon on it, although why they chose a mischievous and bad-tempered Red Dragon to represent their splendid country remains a complete mystery!

Dragon Language

Like every other great species, Dragons have their own language. Theirs is a magical language much too complicated for humans to understand, but this doesn't mean that Dragons are unable to communicate with humankind. Dragons can use their Dragon Magic to make their language understood by any species (not just humans), should they wish to do so (see Dragon Note 7).

But why would a Dragon want to under-stand what humans and other species are saying?

Well, as far as humans and Dragons are concerned, they haven't always been the best of friends, each having a tendency to want to destroy the other. With this in mind, Dragons began to take a keen interest in understanding humans, especially any nasty ones plotting to destroy them!

Dragon Lineage
(The Great Dragon Family Tree)

All Dragons are descended from their Great Dragon Forefather, *FRRROGARR-GWRRRIOORR* which can be roughly translated as Froo-Arggh.

Dragons are born with a complete knowledge of their lineage, able to trace their Great Dragon Family Tree right back to their Great Dragon ancestor, who existed millions of years ago (and many Dragons think still exists).

How Dragons are able to do this is not understood, even by the Dragons them-selves, it's just an ability they are born with.

How Froo-Arggh himself came into existence is part of the Great Universal Mystery.

Many Dragons believe that the Great Dragon was born along with the stars themselves, or even that Froo-Arggh has simply always been in existence (see Dragon Note 8).

෨෬෬

Dragon Note 8

The Draco constellation (or the Dragon constellation), is one of the largest collection of stars prowling the Northern hemisphere skies. Many Dragons believe that Froo-Arggh still lives today and is keeping watch over all Dragonkind.

This concludes our **Brief History of Dragons**. If you would like to know more, it is recommended that you try and get hold of a copy of *Pong's Great Encyclopaedia of Dragonkind: Varieties, Types, Colours and Habitats*, if indeed, any copies still exist.

Good Luck!

Also available from Tomser Cat Books

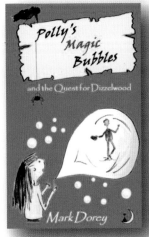

Thank you for purchasing your
Magic Bubbles!
Twelve blows - but not too hard!
Only twelve and no more.
Use your last Bubbles very carefully!
Refunds definitely not available.

Polly and her best friend, Marcia, set out on an incredible adventure, filled with deadly spiders and assassin birds on an amazing quest to Dizzelwood!

and coming Autumn 2016 ...

Spiders! Spiders! Spiders!

Dad's precious pipe has gone missing
Marcia's lost her voice!
Spiders are rampaging everywhere!

Armed with just a bottle of Magic Bubbles and their wits, Polly, with her big brother, Jake, and best friend, Marcia, set out to stop the evil Sor-Ben-Rez and his spider army from taking over the world!

If you have enjoyed reading any of our books

please visit **www.tomsercat.com**

to tell us what you think

and see our other great books too!